The Parkour Code©

By Jay Francis Mistretta
Illustrated by Ryan Gallet
Photography by Andrew Saulnier

ISBN 1-45378-833-6

First Edition
Printed in the U.S.A.
ISBN 1-45378-833-6

TPC Disclaimer

Please seek parental consent and professional guidance when attempting these tricks, maneuvers, and moves.

Rated PG

Parkour Graphamania!

Contents

Chapter 1
Trifecta

Across the planet, on any given day, a parkour jam session involves free-flow action. For Luke Bail and his crew, today isn't any different. Team leader Luke's job is to recruit new talent. To qualify as an X member, a *traceur* or *traceuse* must complete a rigorous boot camp assessment. Finishing a trek brings an athlete one step closer to X status.

"If you want in, keep on moving!" the X leader shouted.

Speed vaulting over a wall and landing on a concrete platform below, Solen hollered, "I want in, man!"

"Now, unleash a Kong vault!" his mentor demanded.

"*Bet!*" the novice traceur replied, diving across a picnic bench. Hitting the dirt below, Sol conducted a side tumble roll.

When the rookie bounced back onto his feet, Luke blasted, "Now, let's jet! This isn't tag. It is a way of life. An X member must keep stepping in order to stay alive. The Westside boys don't play. If they catch us in their territory, we are dealt. Put the hammer down, homey!"

Finishing their jam within about ten minutes, the trek ended downtown at a nearby fashion mall.

"Sweet flow, bro!" Luke assured the senior classmate. "You have some style, kid."

"I'm down with it, man," insisted the novice. "I've learned from Tai chi chuan. My dad has a studio."

"You were shredding it up out there. You have sweet rhythm, kid," the guru praised.

"So, I'm in, right?" the rookie questioned.

"That's a team decision. You need to chill. Now, let's go inside the mall. I need new gear."

While they walked, Luke made his legacy claim to fame. "Parkour is popular around the nation, and opportunities abound. The downturn of the real estate market is creating an ideal situation." He boasted. "New athletes materialize on a weekly basis."

"Cool," Sol replied.

"Unfortunately, there are posers emerging too." The X leader grimaced. "They practice timed sessions and follow-the-leader games." Stopping for a moment and then reconstituting his authoritative stance, he shouted, "My crew is the real deal because we've been trekking these streets for five years!"

"Right on," agreed the newbie.

"We are the street, kid," Luke continued. "We know all the hot spots. We even assign a difficulty level to each jam session, ranking them by name. We call them the black diamond, da' bomb, and the double death. These gigs are when we party. Any jam that isn't ranked is exercise."

"That's a head crash but sounds fresh!" The recruit approved.

"The double death is survival, bro," the captain assured. "We only call it during nine-one-one. Basically, it is when we're in alarm mode being chased by a bug. Trust me, bro, your true skills will erupt in that moment!"

"Did you ever hit death mode?" Sol questioned.

"It only happened a few times," Luke cautiously replied. Pausing to gather his thoughts, he continued. "You don't forget those moments. You either make it or you don't. Your adrenaline will kick in and your instincts take over."

"Did you ever lose someone?" the rookie pried.

"I'd rather not talk about that right now," his mentor insisted. "If and when you reach X status, I'll instruct you in the way of Chung Fu."

As the conversation came to an end, Luke and Solen arrived together at the mall. Entering inside, they scrolled over to the food court. Upon spotting his team, the guru shouted, "It's time for an introduction!" Jabbing Sol, he continued, "This is the new guy. We just finished a trek. He's pretty fly!"

After setting down a deck of playing cards, a traceuse jumped to her feet from behind a table and walked over introducing herself. "Hi, I'm Raven," she replied. "So, you are the new kid, right?"

Slightly perplexed, the recruit didn't answer her question.

"Awe shoot," Raven grumbled. "Here we go again. Yes, I'm a girl!" she affirmed. "Can I ever get respect?"

With the rookie in a verbal bind, Luke didn't want this intro to start off with disrespect. Shouting, the team leader boasted, "She's one of the best on the street!"

"No," Raven disagreed. "I'm the best in the world!" she bragged.

In an attempt to squash the bad vibe, Solen replied, "I believe it!"

"Hey, fool, I'm Jim but you can call me Slim." a sly-looking guy assured. "As for the girl, we call her *Radical* Raven because she rocks!" Jim hooted. "Rave has insane flow!"

"You're in love with her!" Rocco interrupted while bouncing to his feet. "You can't hide it from the rest of us. We know the truth, but she won't give you the time of day."

Slim just grinned. "It's all good!"

Refocusing the group, Luke bellowed, "Let's be for real, people. When we first met Raven, she competed in acrobatics. Although, I think we corrupted her because she left a semi-professional team in order to hang with us."

"You guys are warped!" Raven assured. "I didn't join your crew. You wanted to be my followers. I'm the queen and you are my peasants!"

Calming her down, Rocco whispered, "Now take it easy, darling."

Shaking him off, Raven replied, "Whatever!" Then, looking directly at the new kid, she continued, "So, why are you here?"

With confidence, Sol assured, "Luke invited me."

"No, that isn't what I mean," she corrected. "What do you know about *parkour*?

"Well," the rookie replied, "Parkour is the discipline of training the mind and body to overcome obstacles."

"Okay, what about *freerunning*?" she insisted.

"Um, freerunning is different," Sol noted.

"What do you mean?" Raven interrogated.

"A runner utilizes landscape to perform movement through its structure. By incorporating moves from parkour, an athlete adds creative vaults, tricks, and street stunts over and around obstacles."

"Good," Raven replied. "But, who are you?"

"Alright, let's give the guy a break," Luke interrupted. "Give him the rundown G-man."

Quickly coming to his feet in front of the group, Gordon scanned the room. Smiling at the rookie, he said, "Now let me introduce you to team X. I'll give you the rundown, player! I hope you're the real deal like Luke promotes."

Pointing toward the X captain, Gordon roared, "Let's take a look at specimen number one. This guy is the street king. He's been promoting his gig for years. He has master level skills!"

Then, turning to Raven, the G-man shouted, "Take a look at specimen number two! You think you know her from first glance?" He paused. "Nope, you're wrong. She is one of the most technically sound performers on the planet. Son, I'm talking male and female origin!" he assured. "Yes, we can all duplicate her moves, but she is precise."

Stepping inward, Gordon walked toward Jim. "This Slim

dude over here is crazy smooth. He can run full blast and project his body through the tiniest of crevices. When you bail out on a difficult maneuver, he makes it look easy!"

Then, turning his head to the left toward Rocco, he added, "This dude is our muscle-ninja. He can absolutely rocket and is in perfect physical shape. He gets major air from any launch site. His abdominals are like a washboard. Being our strongman, he's our defensive safety. Rocco will pound you, kid!

Turning back around and stepping toward the rookie, Gordon added, "I'm the watch tower. I'm the backbone of this operation. With Luke's approval, I do the dirty work and make the call on which trek to flow. Nobody moves without me knowing." After an epigrammatic pause, he asked the rookie, "Are you ready to get into the game?"

"Totally," Sol assured.

"Well then, tell us why Luke scouted you. Like Raven was asking, *what you got?*

Slightly distraught, the newbie replied, "I'll tell you what I've got. But first, I need to recap. It's obvious to me that each member has amazing physical ability. As for what I bring, it can make this team better."

"*Really?*" Raven pressed. "Go on."

"I will, but let me backtrack for a moment," the new kid requested. "Obviously, I'm going through an initiation. So, this is how I see it. This team has brains, brawn, adaptability, technical precision, and a pretty cool leader. Do you know what this team needs?"

"What?" Slim inquired.

"*Speed!*" the rookie bellowed.

"Wow, that … wasn't very impressive," Rocco taunted.

Adding to the sentiment, Raven spoke up. "I'm confused. Can you clarify for us?"

"Ouch, that's a slapper!" Jim exclaimed.

Looking past the rebuttal, the recruit continued. "I bring speed. It boosts aerial maneuvers. From what Gordon has told me, all of you are good. You just need speed to make you great!"

"Dude, don't step like that to me, bro," Rocco defended. "I'm the greatest!"

"True, but I've trained with the finest martial artists in America. If you don't believe it, I'll do a demo. I can run a forty yard dash in four point three seconds flat," he boasted. "For me, using momentum creates new moves."

"Show us!" Raven demanded. "You're bluffing," she added. "Prove it right now. This is your chance to be an X member. I won't give you my vote unless you provide me with a demo."

"I'll do it!" Sol replied, excited.

"Over those three barriers," Gordon pointed.

"Come on, everyone, we're in the food court," Luke hollered. "We don't expose ourselves to the public like this!"

"Don't worry about me," the recruit insisted. "I'll do it. You better not blink or you'll miss it!"

"He's lost his mind!" Jim blurted out, shaking his head.

"Here I go!" the recruit announced. Taking off, Solen blasted at full speed toward his first obstacle.

As he took off, Rocco taunted, "He won't make it!"

"He's going to crash," Slim agreed.

Approaching a four-foot-high-by-six-foot-wide concrete wall, the rookie Kong vaulted over it by diving forward headfirst; both arms extended in midair, pushing off the smooth block surface. Upon impacting the cafeteria floor, he then completed a front roll. Within a fraction of a second, Solen sprang upward, turning his body sideways and catapulting vertically toward the roof of the building. Aligning his torso, he performed a speed vault over a large circular wooden table.

Standing erect once again, Solen jetted forward and *Kash* vaulted over an eight-foot high steel fence. Leaping up, he pushed both legs through center over the metal railing. Staying in motion, his body traveled across the open gap of space. His speed took him from the food court into the mall's main lobby. As he rapidly approached the ground, he completed a side shoulder tumble rotation.

When he landed, Luke gasped. "That's a *daisy-chain*!" Solen's flex move caught the X leader off guard.

Bouncing back onto his feet, the rookie decreased his speed and transitioned into a jog. The X had just witnessed Sol complete three maneuvers within a matter of seconds.

"That's high density, bro!" Gordon hooted. "That's a

megabyte!"

"Dude, you rocked it!" Slim agreed.

"For sure, kid," Raven added. "I have to give you props for that."

"Speed rocks!" the rookie restated.

As he spoke, Slim Jim walked over and gave him dap. "Man, teach me those moves, bro. That's fresh!"

"No problem!" Sol assured. "We'll run some gigs."

Interrupting the new kid's moment of bliss, Luke persuaded his team to leave the mall. "I hate to be a party crasher, but we need to dip. We're being spied on. We should get rolling. *Ol'* boy over there is with the Westside. I told you guys that we shouldn't do this here."

Upon his salvo, the X left the mall. Being on site, Raven's vehicle provided a ride back to the neighborhood. During their drive, the teens agreed to meet again at school in order to develop a new jam session. The following day, the crew would congregate inside the gym during third lunch. The team knew that, while in there, Luke occasionally announced a new gig. Always ready for Parkour, the X loved to shred it up inside uncharted territory.

Before getting out of the car, the recruit had one final question. "So, I'm in, right?"

"In unison, the squad replied, "You're in!"

Chapter 2
The X Factor

During third lunch at school the next day, the team gathered on the gym bleachers to debrief, but it quickly turned into a hang out session for most of them. While there, the group carelessly threw around ideas.

With many possible hot spots, Gordon shouted, "It will be off the chain!"

Capturing the moment, Luke stood in front of his friends, reintroducing the initial topic of discussion. "Let's talk business, people! We only have about five minutes before sixth period. Today, we're hitting a jam at five o'clock. Gordon and I have chosen the place because it'll be during the end of the business day. Most people will be too busy to notice a bunch of teens hanging around the downtown area."

Luke paused. "Trust me concerning this hit. This place is a prime location for compiling serious tricked-out conversions. There is an insane menu of activities in store for all of you. While we trek, don't leave your footprint anywhere because this is Westside territory. We need to flow and be precise. I don't want anyone dragging behind." Luke dropped his serious tone for a moment and continued enthusiastically. "We are jamming a black diamond gig! This is the real thing, people. It should be a fairly easy commute. Is everyone clear?"

The team nodded in agreement, ready for action.

"Alright then, I'll text everyone with the information this afternoon. Gear up and peace out!"

After being discharged, the teens left the gym. For the X, a long two hours in class awaited them. They knew it was worth it though to be an X. Luke made sure that his squad knew they had to achieve a high level of academic excellence if they wanted to run gigs. All members maintained at least an average grade in coursework. Attending every class and being on time was mandatory, and no office disciplinary referrals were permitted. In order to trek, you had to be a model student. "If not, you're out," Luke often reminded them. "It's the best way to lose any unwanted attention. Besides, how can you run with us if you're in detention?"

Because of an alternating schedule, the group split between three courses. Jim, Raven, and Gordon were in science class together every Monday and Friday. Solen and Rocco were in history. Luke, on the other hand, partook in automotive design, where he put together small engines. It was his afternoon thrill because he loved mechanical systems.

Each teen was required to choose a field of study during their tenth-grade year, and, as seniors, everyone had to complete a final exam. It was the last door blocking escape to freedom from high school. Unlike the rest of his crew, Luke's final test wasn't on paper. He had to develop a motor from scratch. His assignment was to create a workable concept for a scooter. It had to be designed from scrap metal, but the details didn't matter. He was a genius when it came to building things. With exams in a week, the team's guru couldn't have been happier.

Unfortunately for the rest of the X, they didn't feel the same vibe for their own tests. Thankfully, though, the last semester also ushered in the graduation ceremony. Even with that to look forward to, though, that particular day at that moment, Jim felt the pain.

"Dude, is it three o'clock?" he questioned Gordon. "I've got to get out of here bro!"

Gordon didn't verbally acknowledge his pal. Nonetheless, Jim didn't give up. Trying to get Raven's attention, in the front of the room, he asked, "Where's the text?"

The traceuse didn't respond either, and Slim started to get antsy. While he opened his cell phone to check for the text message, the teacher said firmly, "Young man, please bring me your phone!"

"Oh snap!" Jim replied. After slowly walking to the front of the room, Slim placed the device on the instructor's desk.

"You know the procedure," the teacher admonished with a frown. "I'm giving this phone to your administrator and you must retrieve it from her. You will also spend an hour and a half in detention after school today."

"Dude, do I have to serve detention today?" the sly one inquired. "I only wanted to check the time." When he got no response, he returned to his seat.

Before Slim even made it back to his chair, Luke sent his

text message. When it came through, Jim's phone started buzzing. Although blaring, the teacher pretended not to notice it going off. Flashing across the screen, the X leader's message read, "Meet on Johnson St., the Prestige Computer Institute, @ five." After a few more chirps, the phone stopped humming. Fortunately for him, the front display had flipped upside down and now faced the desktop. Because of it, the classroom instructor never saw the content.

While Jim sat in remorseful disgust, the rest of the squad received Luke's message. Unfortunately, at that point, Gordon and Raven knew their pal would miss the event. Slim's lack of patience had put the team in a negative spotlight.

"Man, what a total spastic maniac!" Gordon grumbled under his breath. "He's definitely off the team."

Not being able to save their teammate, the X would have to move forward as planned. That afternoon's scamper would offer plenty of free flowing action. Gordon knew it. With Luke's help, he had scoped out the site the day before. As visions of a successful trek formed in the G-man's mind, the bell rang, dismissing the class.

"I'll see everyone on Friday," the teacher yelled. "Jim Parker, please head to the dean's office!" he barked. "We have some unfinished business."

Leaving class, Slim glanced over at Raven and Gordon. With a grimace on her face, the traceuse muttered, "You're a punk!"

With this referral, the sly kid had three disciplinary infractions. Although the other two incidents were minor, Slim had let down the team. His violations—one for dress code, one for an unexcused absence, and this one for inappropriate cell phone use—were enough to get him bounced from the X squad. Not able to justify the situation, Slim knew that Luke would become volcanic concerning this careless mistake.

"Tell the rest of the team that I'm sorry," Jim repented.

"Whatever!" The traceuse rebutted.

Without further debate, Gordon said, "It's our time, slacker. We'll catch you later." Then, pulling Raven with him down the hall, the G-man enlightened her concerning the event. "PCI has plenty of obstacles to hoax. The abandoned building sits on an acre of land. There's plenty of heavy equipment to trick out. It is going to be the perfect landing site!"

"That sounds cool," she replied. "Let's get out of here and go to my house because we still have time. Besides, I need to get my gear."

While darting to the parking lot, Gordon spotted Jim and shouted, "Knucklehead!" Turning to Raven, he added, "He just makes me so mad."

"I know," the traceuse agreed. "Don't worry about it now though. Let's jet."

"Right on," he approved.

The teens headed to the school's front lot, where Raven's truck was parked. Meanwhile, as they left campus, Solen and

Rocco searched for Luke and eventually located him inside the automotive academy, where he was cleaning up his area. When he'd finished, the three teens left via the rear student lot and loaded into Luke's supercharged automobile. Upon hitting the street, the car's engine roared with strength and prestige.

"This is a sweet ride," Solen approved. "This is a real finder, bro!"

"True!" Luke concurred. "I adjusted the engine in the auto shop. I'm also thinking of adding some nitrous. If I do, this car will launch!" he bragged.

"For sure, kid!" Rocco replied. "I've modified cars before. This thing will rocket!" he guaranteed.

"I'll be able to surge!" Luke proclaimed.

"This car will be nuclear!" Sol reiterated. "It'll go from *drag to drop*!"

Dishing out verbal accolades, the X zoomed to the downtown area. Arriving at the PCI building within twenty minutes, Luke pulled the car into the first floor garage and smoothly parked the vehicle.

Turning off the vehicle, Luke twisted his keys to allow the radio to play while the engine was off. Listening to music before a trek was his typical procedure. The music eased his mind.

"That's a classic," Rocco announced. "Turn it up!"

After a few songs, the guru completely shut the car off, and the three traceurs unloaded into the vacant parking lot.

"It's an ideal launch!" Rocco said excitedly.

"*Bet!*" the guru concurred. "This will be our starting point for the jam. Hey, while we wait for the others, why don't we go and explore?"

"Cool," Solen replied. "Let's do it!"

"I'm down with that," Rocco confirmed.

Navigating away from the parking facility, the three members attempted to score preview points. While walking the site, the teens checked the outer rim of the entire lot. By doing so, they could uncover any hidden danger. Without preplanning, Luke knew a group of thugs would easily overpower his crew. On every gig, the X split into small groups. Although a risky decision, it became a common practice to only have two or three athletes on a single flow. For that reason, defending against a large scale attack was difficult.

"The Westside have deep roots in the area," the X leader warned. "I've had plenty of nasty encounters with them. It can get ugly out here." Having flashbacks, he continued, "Honestly, I still get a little spooked on new treks. To stay safe, always check your rearview mirror."

"Why are you crashing my database, kid?" Rocco questioned.

"Yeah, I was ready up until now!" the rookie admitted.

"I'm talking smack," Luke teased. "Don't worry about it because I'm just decompressing. We'll be fine."

"Well, thanks for *scaring!*" Solen winced.

"Oh, by the way, I almost forgot to mention the most important thing," the guru confessed. "I didn't tell you about our emergency response yet."

"What is it?" the rookie replied.

Luke responded, "It's our *control-alt-delete*."

Piping up, Rocco added, "It's our reboot, man!"

"Yes, exactly," agreed the X leader. He clarified, "Whenever it's time to bailout on a gig, we call *creeper*!" If you hear that word, you need to get out. Run as fast as you can. Be back at my house within fifteen minutes. My crib is the buffer zone."

"What if someone doesn't make it back?" Solen asked.

"Rescue mission!" Rocco interjected. "Someone has to voluntarily go back in and save you!"

"Yeah, that's how it goes down," Luke agreed. "From my experience, if you're not in the zone within fifteen minutes, it's a bad code."

"What's a bad code?"

"Let me give you the run down," Rocco replied. "A bad code means that the street cancer got to you. By the time you are located, you've either been jumped, ambushed, or both. If it is an arrest, then law enforcement called a *code two*. If under arrest, you did something really stupid. Police officers typically allow parkour in public areas. If any of these things happen to you during a trek, it proves that you aren't professional. If you get trapped, escape. If we have to *save* you, it means that you are weak. Getting caught will jeopardize your existence. Your system will be frozen because Luke will bounce you from the X squad!" he promised. "That means no more gigs, man," Rocco added.

When the team's strongman finished his verbal volley, the scouting session ended. Half-baked from the *creeper* conversation, the rookie walked with his pals to the parking lot. At that moment, Sol realized that parkour was a way of life for the X team.

"Your first real gig starts today," Rocco reminded.

Snapping out of his funk, the rookie replied, "Let's do it!"

"It's almost go time, kid," his mentor assured.

Just then, Raven and Gordon pulled up to the building. The traceuse parked her truck inside the garage. As she and Gordon got out of the vehicle, Luke shouted, "All clear for trekking!" Then, with a confused look on his face, he inquired, "Where's Slim?"

When Raven didn't respond, the X leader shouted, "I'll take care of it later. Now, let's roll!"

Chapter 3
The Black Diamond

"Go!" Luke shouted.

Upon his authorization, the X instantly scattered. Separating into two teams, each group carved out a different trek. Solen found himself following quickly behind Luke, heading toward the rear of the building, where the two traceurs ran a course straight through the center of the facility. As their flow erupted, the teens vaulted and leaped over commercial equipment, clearing obstacles.

In order to get to the heart of the building, the X leader and his recruit bypassed debris. Maneuvering over a five-foot aluminum flex fence, they utilized more upper-body strength and swung both legs skyward. From there, they twisted back around and landed on the ground conducting a basic dive roll. Popping to their feet, they dashed toward the facility.

Meanwhile, as Luke and Sol leapt ahead, Raven led her group straight into the center of the yard. Dashing toward a wall, she found a large air conditioning unit pressed up against it. With one step, she pounced on top. By pushing off the metal surface, the traceuse completed a cat leap toward a windowsill and managed to grab the white sill. Her forward momentum helped her swing both feet wide and parallel with the building's concrete block. Springing her legs upward, Raven flowed into the next move. After completing a personalized side boomerang twist, she pulled herself to the top level. At that point, the traceuse stood up. Tucking her head and completing a shoulder-to-hip side roll, Raven disappeared into the shadows of the building. Following quickly behind, Rocco and Gordon employed a similar technique. The G-man trailed Raven while the strongman ran caboose.

While her crew blasted into the structure, Luke and his trainee shuffled across a pipe for about ten yards. Then, using an under bar grab, the X leader propelled his body through on open window. The rookie completed the same trek.

Entering a room on the bottom level, Sol noticed his mentor picking up speed. Turning on the jets, the recruit caught his pal in a flash. As soon he did, the guru tricked a Kong vault, diving over an elongated black leather office couch. As soon as he'd landed on the carpet, Solen mimicked his move.

Utilizing a Dyno, Luke then grabbed an overhang. His velocity brought the jam session upward. Finalizing his flow, the guru exploded across an open threshold into an arm jump toward the crossbars on the second story. Grabbing the upper railing, he pulled himself skyward. When he did, Solen copycatted that maneuver, too.

"Rip it up, dude!" the X leader shouted.

In order to get to the upper level, both teens had to glide through midair. In no time at all, with a few simple maneuvers, they catapulted themselves to the top deck. Upon hitting that elevation, both athletes navigated their way down a hall.

"*Sweet!*" Solen bellowed.

"Keep flowing, kid!" Luke commended.

At that moment, unbeknown to anyone in the building, danger brewed. It was more than just a rival teenage crew— darkness had seeped into their city. Although the X knew that anything could happen while trekking, they didn't anticipate a bigger threat than the Westside. Today, fortunately, the darkness didn't expose itself. Luke and Sol blasted forward without interruption. They established fluid movement on the second floor in the direction of Raven's team. As they approached the center of the building, Solen spotted Rave, Rocco, and the G-man ready to pull off the coolest transitional moves that afternoon.

Getting Luke's attention Sol shouted, "Check it!"

"It's the grand finale!" Raven hooted.

In order to make it a radical day, she approached the stairs first. Then, exploding from the top entrance of the brass spiral staircase, Raven struck the mahogany post with a few short hops. Placing her hands over her head, she unleashed a shoulder abduction move. While gripping the handrail, the traceuse punched the floor with her feet, which shot her legs upward into the air at point. With legs overhead, Raven then used a precise counterturn to change direction and enter a switch stance. With legs dangling above, she finished with a Salto dismount.

Instantly flipping back into a goofy foot upright position, Raven surfed the apex railing. While on top of the iron banisters, she traveled all the way down to the floor. At the bottom, when it was time to bail out, she completed an aerial front flip, landing on both feet. Her forward crescent roll softened the tumble, and she bounced back up from the tile floor just in time to see Gordon's performance.

"Hit it dude!" she yelled to her pal.

From a distance, Solen also shouted, "Holy smoke, did you see that?"

While he gawked, Gordon hit his mark on the wood post. He completed a palm spin without clearance. The three-hundred-sixty-degree revolving tornado rotation returned him to his initial position within seconds. Without delay, the G-man placed both hands on the banister about shoulder width apart. Then, with just enough room to squeeze his sneaker inside, he inserted his right foot into the hollowed side railing loop. Swinging his left leg upward, he placed his other foot on the top railing. Finally, in order to build friction, he slid all the way down to the bottom utilizing a skater's grind technique. Instantly transforming his grind into a modified leg grab, he launched over the end post treating the rail as a catapulting mechanism.

"Wahoo!" he hollered.

After shooting outward and being airborne, Gordon completed a diving roll. Landing on the ground, he then launched to his feet like a superhero.

"Wow, you're amazing!" the recruit hollered.

Gordon turned toward the stairway in anticipation of Rocco's first move. With a smooth surge, the team's strongman completed an adaptation of a squat box jump. After leaping over the side railing, approximately four feet high, Roc spun his entire body around. The one-hundred-eighty-degree rotation caused him to face inward toward the staircase. While in midair, he grabbed the guardrail at the same moment that both feet landed on the *outside* extended step of the stairwell. Standing there, on the outer platform, he then gripped the thin metal balustrade. Releasing his footing, Rocco used his own body's weight to pull him downward.

"Go rock star!" Luke shouted from above.

Outside the stairwell, gripping the balustrade, Rocco descended. Upon reaching the edge of the outer rung, he swung his left arm inward and grabbed the step from *underneath*. Then, pulling his right arm over, Rocco dangled above the ground.

"What the heck?" the rookie yelped.

Appling his own inventive genius, Rocco transitioned the flight of stairs *from below*.

"Say what?" Luke freaked.

Without wavering, the ironman descended using a hand-under-hand maneuver. Swinging each arm in a semicircular motion, his body traversed downward. Like climbing monkey bars, Rocco's core strength controlled his side to side sway.

"Is he for real?" Raven gasped.

With a sudden pause, Roc stopped within eight feet of the floor. Pulling his feet toward his hands, he rolled both legs between his arms. Pushing off, he completed a back flip and landed on the tile.

"Oh snap!" the rookie hollered. "That's unbelievable, bro!"

"Thanks, man," Rocco replied. "It's your turn, player."

Upon cue, the rookie took center stage. He darted toward an open loft. With Luke following closely behind, Solen ran directly at a two-inch-thick tempered glass enclosure. Approaching it, the recruit completed a wall flip by pushing off the lower frame. Before turning over, his hands contacted its top surface, stabilizing his body. Back on his feet once again, he turned and sprang to a nearby platform. Leaping outward and extending his legs, he landed on an offset adjacent atrium about five feet below the second floor. Via a displacement roll, he softened the blow.

After tumbling forward, Sol almost smashed himself into an adjoining solid block barrier wall. Being decisive, he quickly transitioned a low level Tic-Tac pushing off the wall's surface with the ball of his right foot. After shifting across the exterior, the recruit finished off the jam session by soaring skater style toward the first floor. In mid flight, by setting both heels at a forty-five degree angle, he shifted his weight upright. As soon as he did, Solen pulled off a *Japan air,* scoring points with the crowd.

"Nice!" the traceuse raved.

At that point, the rookie completed a precision jump and sprang toward a table. Touching down together on top, his shoes *then* hop scotched across. The momentum propelled Sol forward until he jumped from the table and landed on the ground. Following directly behind him, Luke silhouetted his pal.

"That's ripping!" Raven howled.

"Sweet flow, bro!" Rocco agreed.

"You're styling!" Gordon smiled.

"*Bet!*" the new kid cheered.

Upon landing his dismount, Luke decided to end the X session. Quickly eighty-sixing the gig, he proclaimed, "It's been fun but now it's time to jet. We need to dip before things go south. Let's cruise back to my place."

After leaving the office building, the team strolled toward the parking lot.

"Hey, we just finished a black diamond, true?" Sol inquired.

"Luke gave you the rundown, right?" Raven questioned.

"He told me that there is a black diamond, da' bomb and a double death."

"Listen, bro," Raven snickered. "First, the name of the trek isn't its location. It is the level of difficulty. Next, there are only two degrees of complexity. This is a black diamond. The other jam is called *da'* bomb."

"What about the double death?" the rookie persisted.

"Dude, the double death can happen anytime," Rave explained. "That mode is called *creeper.* The double death can be called during any flow."

"Why double death?"

The other members finally jumped into the conversation.

"There are two ways to get crushed!" Rocco pointed out. "Dude, you can die twice."

Gordon interjected. "The street melanoma is the first death. If the Westside don't finish you off, we are your second."

"We end your program, kid," Raven concurred. "You're no longer on our squad."

"Like I mentioned before, your stellar career would be over," Luke added, "if you got caught!"

"If you don't make it out, you're a goner," Raven concluded. "We don't know you."

The conversation dropped as soon as the squad spotted Slim Jim approaching the lot.

"Dude, go home!" Luke shouted.

"Let me explain!" the sly one insisted.

"No!" the guru rebuked. "You need to leave.

For a moment, neither teen spoke, and an awkward stare down transpired. After a few seconds, Jim honored Luke's request and walked away.

"It's my bad, captain!" Slim yelled while leaving the lot.

As he departed, Raven openly disapproved of how Luke had handled the situation. "Do you call that executive authority?" she protested. "You didn't do anything to him!"

"I'll handle it!" Luke blasted. "We aren't doing this here. I'll take care of it tomorrow."

Unsatisfied with his reply, the traceuse rebutted, "But—"

"Drop it!" Luke shouted. Hastily changing the topic, he yelled, "Now, let's jet."

Zipping off the lot, the X journeyed back to Luke's house. Arriving there, the squad discussed their black diamond gig.

"It was a gnarly time, man!" Rocco celebrated while retracing the events of that day.

Going around the room, each member shared a noteworthy experience, and everyone bragged about his or her personal stellar performance. It had been a sweet trek. After two hours of recap, before parting ways, the X planned to regroup at school the following day.

"Be at the gym during third lunch," Luke reminded.

Chapter 4
The Summer Plan

"Where is that punk?" Luke questioned, shoving classmates out of his way.

Taking care of business, the master traceur tried catching Jim before breakfast. Navigating down a corridor, he spotted Slim at his locker. Pouncing on his friend, the X leader shoved Sly into a storage room.

"Bro, get your act straight!" Luke threatened.

"I will!" Jim promised. "I just need to focus."

"Man, you know the rules. We don't need a jester on this team!"

"I'm sorry, bro," Slim apologized.

"This is your last chance, kid!" Luke swore.

"Okay, I won't mess around anymore."

"If you mess up again, you're out!"

"I won't," Slim promised again.

Following the intense skirmish, the X captain invited Jim to the forum that day.

"Sure, I'll be there."

At lunch dismissal, the guru located his pal and together they entered the gymnasium. To show that he was backing his friend, Luke purposely walked Slim to the bleachers.

"Nice to see you, man," Raven taunted.

"Give him a break. We spoke this morning. He's

straight," replied the team's guru.

"Sure, he'll be a model student," Raven muttered.

Ignoring the dispute, Gordon commenced the meeting. "Hey, I searched the Internet last night," he announced.

"Yeah, no kidding, that's all you do," Rocco countered. "I can track your progress from my house. You live on your ‚computer, bro!"

Saving face, the G-man shot back with, "If you're viewing my status, you must be on it, too!" Waving him off, he continued with, "Anyway, I found a radical parkour facility!"

"Is it in Mexico?" the rookie asked.

"Mexico?" the Gordon replied. "Are you feeling alright?" He questioned. "Dude, we live in Florida. The park is in Europe!" He assured. "Anyhow, the facility just opened and is considered the world's largest trekker location!"

It's in Denmark," Luke added. "It's the new hot spot in Copenhagen."

"Yeah, that's the location!" the G-ster shouted. "The park's design is inspired by some of the best artists on earth. It boasts of a multi-dynamic platform.

"Are you for real?" Solen asked.

"This is no joke, bro!" Gordon assured. "A landscape architect completed the blueprints. Beside that, a well-known local crew created its layout. It took a lot of outside funding to get started. This place has serious compression!"

"It sounds dope!" Raven bellowed.

"Right on," agreed Rocco. "It sounds ripping! We have to go there man!"

"We absolutely need to go there," the G concurred. "There is only one problem though. The park is located thousands of miles away. If we're going, we need a plan, folks. This is the big time!"

"Let's do it!" Luke announced. "Let's go this summer!"

"Yeah, that's the ticket, baby!" Slim hollered. "It's almost the end of the school year, right?" he reminded them. "If we all work full-time during June and July, we can save enough money to go in August. What do you all think about that?"

"I'm in!" Raven guaranteed.

"Count me in, too!" the new kid echoed.

"Let's do it!" the X leader shouted. "It'll be our summer trek!"

"Definitely," agreed Gordon. "Dude, this park is radical!" Pausing to collect his thoughts, he continued, "They spent a half million dollars and two and a half years of hard work building this parkour fortress!"

Luke quickly began chalking out a plan. "First, we need money in order to buy airfare. That's the expensive part. After that, we'll book a hotel room."

"What about the passports?" Raven interrupted.

"Yes, we also need identification. We can't travel internationally without that," he added.

"What about transportation?" Solen pried.

"We can take a cab to the airport," he assured them. "In Europe, we'll travel via train and metro. I'll work out the details and get more info later," he concluded.

"What do you think about going the first week in August?" Raven proposed.

"That sounds good to me," agreed Slim.

"It's Copenhagen or bust!" the recruit clamored. "We're taking a summer trip!"

"Alright then, calm down," Luke said. "I'll arrange everything." Snapping back to reality he added, "As for today, it's time to get to class. I'm planning a big trek this weekend. I'm busy during the week, but we can meet at my house on Saturday at seven in the morning. At that time, I'll provide everyone with the new location. It'll be a dangerous place, so gear up and be ready! It'll be the da' bomb!"

"Say what!" Raven hooted.

"Yes, this is the big time. I'll reveal the location on Saturday," he reiterated. "Peace out!"

With a new gig proposed, the X left for class. For all of them, that school day ended quickly. That afternoon Luke and Gordon scoped out an old junkyard site. Unfortunately, inside, they discovered two devilish dogs guarding the premises. They could tell that the trained canines monitored the property. Because of it, the gig could bring the squad to the breaking point.

"Dude, this is the biggest jam we've ever hit!" Gordon stated.

"I know," Luke replied.

"Are you sure about it?"

"Don't bail out on me, kid. I need you to be strong." Luke didn't waver. Knowing the site was extreme, he remained vigilant.

"This place is unbearable!" Gordon insisted. "Look at all the debris. That giant stack of rubber tires is insane. And what about all those abandoned vehicles?" he added. "Man, this yard has broken glass and rusty parts all over it. Someone is going to get slashed."

"Well, it isn't a place for the fainthearted," the guru agreed.

"It's a dangerous trek, man!" Gordon protested.

"Yes, it's extreme, but are you in or out?" Luke inquired.

"I'm in!" the G-man replied. "Let's do it!"

After scouting the area, the G and his advisor left. For the X waiting for Saturday's jam, the rest of that week evolved rapidly. That Friday night, at home, the rookie scrambled to put his gear together for the session. Trying on a pair of athletic sneakers, he looked for traction that provided grip for street action and granted little space for toe movement. Being durable, he chose shoes with flexible synthetic material that didn't compromise safety. Although lightweight, they provided cushion support.

As for clothing, he had to consider a few options, not knowing what the weather would be.

"First, storm attire," he said to himself. Scanning his closet, he located a tight shirt and baggy pants in a strong lightweight material.

Each night before a jam, the novice rehearsed his technique. Utilizing his martial arts training, he stretched and unwound his mind and body and unleashed any tension. Within a fifteen minute workout, the recruit was prepared for a trek.

Meanwhile, as Sol practiced his routine, the X boss sat at home mentally equipping himself for the gig. That evening, the team's captain wrestled with a legal issue. For the most part, performing parkour in public places was permitted by law enforcement. A traceur or traceuse could compete in most locations. The junkyard was different, though. If the gates were locked, the X would need to clear the fence. If they did, the event would be considered illegal. Although the yard was an outrageously insane engagement, entering the property when it was closed could result in a felony charge.

Still, Luke tried to visualize a positive outcome by verbally disputing his case. Wresting with emotion, he pondered, "I know it is wrong. We have to do it because it's da' bomb, man. But, what if we get caught?" he questioned himself. "I'll be putting the team in jeopardy. I always tell them do the right thing. Oh man, but this is big time. Maybe this whole idea is a big mistake?"

Suddenly, Luke had an epiphany. Excited, Luke stated, "It's all about timing! Instead of getting to the yard while it's closed, we'll jam after it opens. By doing so, we won't get in trouble with the cops. If we're caught, the store owner will see us as a bunch of teenagers playing around, not criminals breaking and entering."

Having a renewed sense of direction, Luke also realized that arriving at the junkyard after it opened meant no threatening canines. "Hopefully, by that time, the owner will have chained the dogs to their cage. Without them, there is one less variable to factor into the equation," the guru concluded.

Now, with a plan in place, Luke dozed off. Morning seemed to arrive quickly with its new day of adventure. While gearing up, the X leader heard a knock at his front door and opened it to find Gordon.

"Are you ready to jam?"

"I'm absolutely ready!" Luke howled.

The rest of the X approached, and after a brief team gathering on the driveway, the teens scampered into the house. Challenging Luke, Rocco probed, "By now, we could have been halfway to the site, bro. Are you feeling alright, captain?"

"That's right!" Raven agreed. "What's up?"

"I'm straight," Luke insisted. I just need to make sure everyone is ready. Today is a big day!"

"I'm ready to flow, chief!" Solen announced.

"Count me in!" Slim replied.

"Alright then, here's the scoop. We are jamming the old junkyard on county line just outside of town." After a pause to gauge reactions, he continued. "Yes, we are going to see Jack!"

"Oh shoot, brother!" Rocco protested. "Man, I heard that they have dogs out there."

"True!" Gordon interrupted. "But, it's an elite hot spot!" he guaranteed.

"If you're not down with it, you can leave now," Luke interjected.

"No, I'm cool," Rocco replied.

The team's lack of excitement upset the X leader. In frustration, he busted out with, "I'm giving everyone one last chance. If you are dropping out, leave now!"

"We're all in!" Raven pledged. "Run your script leader-man. We need details."

"Well, here's the rundown," he replied. "The site is hazardous. If the dogs are locked up, it'll be a smoother session. If not, move faster. In the yard, there is a ton of debris. Trick it out!" He smiled. "Don't forget that tires are a distraction. Utilize them carefully. They are unstable and will crash your flow. Keep moving in order to survive! Are we straight?"

"Serve it up!" Gordon shouted. "Let's do this!"

"It's time to ride!" Raven prompted. "Let's move!"

Cramming into Luke's vehicle, the X jetted down the highway and reached the yard in about ten minutes. As they approached their destination, Luke parked his car one block from the facility. The crew crossed the road toward Jack's sliding metal front gate. As soon as it hit eight o'clock, the X leader hollered, "Look the business is open!" With the locks off and gate open, Luke proclaimed, "It's time to jam! We're going in three teams of two. Be on the lookout for *creeps*. Be alert, but rip it up. I'll be trekking with Gordon. We're going deep through the middle. We are team three." Then, turning toward Rocco, he directed, "You are team two. Take Slim with you and don't leave him behind. Travel the north side where the machinery is located." Finally, pointing at Raven, he concluded, "You are team number one. Take the new guy with you. Hike the south side nearest the building."

"What about our exit?" Raven requested. "What's the plan?"

"Everyone will surge to the opposite side of the facility. Then, trek back to my car in thirty minutes." In a final farewell the X leader shouted, "It's time to party!"

Chapter 5
Junkyard Dog

Crossing the road, the X split into teams of two as directed. Raven took off and headed to the south side of the lot with Solen tailing behind. Turning down a grungy dirt path, the first team evaded rusty car parts by hurdling them.

"Let's hit the line closest to the wall!" the rookie yelled ahead.

"Cool," agreed the traceuse.

While they pursued that trail, Rocco grabbed Jim and blasted in the opposite direction toward the north side of the facility. In a spurt, the teens leaped, twisted, and vaulted over stacks of plastic bumpers, metal fenders, and rubber tires.

Pointing, Rocco shouted, "Dude, let's rip on that old car carrier!"

Giving two thumbs up, Slim replied, "Yeah man!"

Approaching the car loader, the teens noticed its loading bed didn't hold any vehicles. Because of it, the traceurs zoomed through the platform rapidly performing bar-grab maneuvers.

Waiting until everyone dispersed, the team leader grabbed Gordon, and together they jetted straight through the heart of the yard. Unlike the rest of the squad, their path became the main artery. Unbeknown to them, the overabundant automobiles preceded the segment housing the junkyard dogs.

As team three hit their first row of automobiles, both the

guru and the G dove across the hood of a vehicle, utilizing a waist high Kong vault. Bouncing off the ground, they sprang back into action, darting directly toward a stack of double high wrecks. In order to maneuver between them, the teens Tic-Tacked across each metal tailgate. Within a matter of seconds, Luke transitioned a truck's synthetic bumper and performed a modified spring vault. Spiraling upward, he catapulted to the upper level ten feet above the ground. Utilizing the same technique, Gordon elevated himself to the top.

"Hey, bro, let's cat leap across!" Luke hollered.

"Yeah, that's the ticket!" Gordon hooted. "Let's blast!"

While they soared from above, Raven and Sol slithered in and out of a narrow passageway. Enclosed between a wall on one side and a large pile of trash on the other, the teens athleticism erupted.

"Rip it up!" the rookie bellowed.

"You wish you could keep up with me, kid," Raven boasted.

After vaulting over an empty oversized aluminum chemical barrel, the traceuse turned a corner. When she did, Solen dashed in the same direction. Unfortunately, however, he didn't spot the container. At that moment, missing his mark, the rookie crashed to the earth all busted up. His left foot cleared the obstacle but his right didn't. Scrapping the metal drum, his forward momentum halted. The snag sent him tumbling down into the dirt. Using both hands, he braced for impact. Upon contacting the ground, his chest bounced skyward.

"Whoa!" Sol gasped trying to regain his composure. "Ouch!" He winced, impacting the dirt once more.

Attempting to save face, he completed a forward summersault front roll. Regaining equanimity, the new kid then stood on his feet.

"That sucked!" he admitted. Glancing at a small gash on his leg, he added, "Oh man, that's wicked!"

Notwithstanding the cut, Sol's overall shock turned out to be worse than the actual plummet. Standing alone, the rookie contemplated the reason for entering into crash mode. He knew the answer. Scrawled across the exterior wall of Jack's building was a colorful display of graffiti of every sort. Various spray painted signs and symbols covered the entire concrete block. Intrigued, the rookie had jeopardized his safety with lack of focus, letting the art and diverse style of font become his distraction.

Glancing at an unknown marking, he pondered aloud, "What *is* that?" Capturing Sol's curiosity, one symbol stood out more than the rest. Fiddling with his cell phone, he quickly snapped a photo. "That sign is definitely different. I've never seen anything like it before."

Refocusing his attention back to reality, Solen checked his battle wound. Then, also taking a picture of it, he added the snapshot to the phone's media directory. Finally, after conducting a brief manic photography session, he finished the shoot by loading, sorting, and saving the pics into his device. Before putting the gadget away, the recruit e-mailed the images to the other X members.

Finally, recalling the mission's original objective, Solen blasted off in order to locate Raven. If it weren't for the face plant, his jam that day would have been an amazing trek.

While the recruit searched for the team's traceuse, Rocco and Slim ripped on the car carrier. They utilized a diverse range of arm bar grabs in order to maneuver in and out of the trailer. Occasionally, gripping a steel shaft, they whipped around in a full three-hundred-and-sixty-degree rotation. Often unable to slow down, they spun out of control. The extra twirling didn't matter.

"It's a good time!" Roc boasted.

Giving a shout out, Slim named the maneuver "The killer vortex."

When only conducting a half rotation, the traceurs released their grip from the metal frame. By launching high in the air, they could conduct a flying summersault.

"Wahoo!" Rocco shouted.

Transitioning to a Dyno, the boys then extended upward and outward in the direction of a bar higher than themselves. By doing so, the teens were able to perform major tricks in midair. Without an audience, they turned into acrobatic gymnasts on the uneven bars.

"Dude, check me out!" Jim hollered. "I'm sky high!"

While team two corrupted the abandoned carrier, Luke

and Gordon played aerial patrol. Standing on a car's hood on the upper deck, the X leader started launching from one vehicle's hood to the next. When he did, the G piggybacked his maneuver. Too busy free flowing forward, team three didn't noticed the dog house five rows ahead. After utilizing a cat leap, the X leader gestured to the G-man and shouted, "Move onward!"

While transitioning from above, the teenagers catapulted from one automobile to the next. By bringing both legs in and then kicking them out again, they sprang directly at a vehicle's fortified doorframe. Landing just above each door handle, their shoes absorbed the initial blow. Avoiding windows, the athletes leaped like jackrabbits with unparalleled human strength.

"I'm soaring!" the G roared.

"I'm invincible!" the X leader boasted.

Then, out of the blue, a soul-piercing bark changed everything. Its deep percussion resonated and shook the entire lot. The barking quickly became louder. Like a trumpet, the fierce canine alarm blasted. Both dogs raged in full throttle. Taking Luke and Gordon by surprise, the barking almost made them fall headfirst on the doghouse.

"Whoa, dude!" the G-man shrieked.

"We almost got chomped!" Luke screeched.

Now officially in retreat, the X captain and his pal quickly transitioned to an isle of cars in order to get away. Leaping across the isle, they the jumped to the ground and started running. After trekking over one more set of vehicles, the teens forged a path directly toward the main gate.

"Sound the alarm, man!" Gordon hollered.

"*Creeper!*" Luke yelled. "*Creeper!*" he shouted once more.

The rest of the crew immediately heard Luke's wailing siren.

"*Creeper!*" he bellowed. "*Creeper!*"

Although Luke's voice was a little shaky, the word spread like wildfire once his announcement rang out.

While guru and G-mister ran for freedom, Rocco and Slim stopped in their tracks.

"It's time to jet!" Rocco prompted.

"Let's go!" Slim agreed.

Like buzzing bees, they exited the yard and raced straight toward Luke's car.

While they ran, Raven scrambled, trying to get herself into gear. Turning, in the opposite direction, she barreled back down the narrow passageway. Practically running directly into Solen, the queen almost got herself dethroned.

"Hold up, homey!" she warned.

Nearly flattening her, the new kid squealed, "Look out!"

Shoving him away from her just in time, she bellowed, "We're in *creeper* and need to get out of here!"

"Let's boot!" he replied.

Like missiles blasting from a launch pad, team one jettisoned along the dirt trail. Determined to make it to the front gate, they both dove behind a pile of rubber tires when Raven spotted Jack stepping out into the yard.

"Get down!" the traceuse yelled.

While ducking behind debris, Sol and Rave watched as their pals charged past the gate beyond the business owner.

In a state of shock, Jack shouted, "Stay off my property, you darn kids!"

Making a beeline toward Luke's vehicle, the four boys didn't look back. Pouring into the street, they disappeared.

"I'm calling the cops," the owner promised. "You better not come back!" he added.

While he yelled, Raven and Solen painfully transitioned forward behind a mountain of scrap metal. Sitting frozen in fear, about one hundred feet from the yard's exit, the teens watched while the proprietor bellowed.

"Next time, I'll sick the dogs on you!" the owner promised. "You stay out of here!"

After making his last threat, Jack went back into the office lobby. Although he had left, team one still felt trapped among the rubble.

"I think he's gone," Sol assured.

"I don't have a good feeling about this," the traceuse complained.

"Maybe we should just run for the gate?" the rookie suggested.

"I'm not sure about that," Raven replied.

"Don't worry, I'll lead us out," swore the recruit. "When we get to a clearing, haul butt to Luke's car. Run as fast as you can!"

Taking initiative, Solen inched his way toward the gate's opening. With his female team member shadowing him, the rookie weaved in between rusty auto parts. After completing a tuck roll and low vault, he came upon a clearing.

Informing Raven, he whispered, "There's the gate."

"You go first," she insisted.

Taking off, Sol sprang into action. While running, his heart raced and his mind went into sensory overload. Upon reaching the gateway, he turned to see if Raven tagged behind him. His heart sank when he saw she wasn't. "Oh snap! Oh no," he moaned.

Quickly reacting, the recruit changed direction. From the street, he blasted back toward the yard's entrance. Then, darting toward the building, he hid by pressing his shoulder blades against the facility's front office concrete wall. While standing there in desperation, Solen considered his options. Gathering his thoughts, he declared to himself, "It's time to order car parts!"

The Killer Vortex

Chapter 6
Rescue Mission

Without considering his own safety, Solen opened Jack's main office front door. Strolling inside, he approached the customer service desk and rang the patron bell.

Coming from a back room, Jack inquired, "How can I help you?"

Stumbling over his words, the rookie requested, "I need some of those."

"What do you need?" the owner questioned. "Some of those …" He swallowed, unable to finish. "Hey kid, if you're soliciting for a school fundraiser, I don't have any money to give you. Please take your business elsewhere."

Building up his confidence, the youthful patron replied, "No sir, I'm not here for that."

"Well, what are you here for then?" the business man probed once again.

"Sir, I need car parts," replied Solen.

"Why didn't you say so, son?" Jack perked up. "I have all kinds. What kind of car is it?"

"It's a blue oldie," the teen replied.

"That's an interesting vehicle," Jack snickered.

"It's called a Volkswagen," the adolescent persisted. "It was built in nineteen seventy."

"Sure, I know that year and model. That little hotrod is a

lot of fun. What parts do you need?"

Sol wasn't familiar with common auto components. Winging it, he said, "I need a right fender, front grill, and two headlights."

"Great!" Jack replied. "Well, I place the older vehicles in the back. I'm pretty sure that I'll have everything you need. Let's go check them out," he suggested.

In order to provide Raven more time to escape, Solen played along by suggesting, "Sir, can you give me a price first?"

Slightly baffled, Jack interjected, "Well, most people want to see the parts first before I run the numbers. Don't you want to see what I have?"

"No, as long as they're in fair condition, I'll buy them," Sol assured.

"Alright, kid, I'll check my computer database."

While the storeowner calculated, the rookie peered through a window into the yard. Even with a slightly obscured view, the recruit spotted Raven in the lot hiding behind a monster truck tire.

Attempting to stall for more time, the novice blurted aloud, "Hey, did you know that my car is special?"

In bewilderment, the owner replied, "Sure thing kid." After a pause, he added, "Actually, I know all about your Volkswagen. I restored one and it's in my back warehouse." Completing taking over the conversation, he rattled on, "During nineteen seventy, everything changed on the vehicle. It received a new sixteen hundred four-cylinder air-cooled upgraded engine. It may not sound like much, but its horsepower was cranked to fifty-seven. Besides that, the motor was mounted in the rear of the vehicle in order to provide traction for the back wheels. By doing so, it made the bug relatively easy to maintain."

Half engaged in the conversation, Solen pretended to listen to Jack's story. "Wow that sounds cool. Er … What color are the parts?"

"Well, once again son, we need to check the lot," Jack pointed out." Still navigating on his computer, he carried on about ten minutes on how a nineteen seventy Volkswagen had fine qualities. "Oh yes!" he clamored. "The car featured large turn signals and taillights with side reflectors."

"That's cool," the teen agreed.

While the Volkswagen fanatic babbled, Raven spotted Solen and recognized the rescue mission. She realized that the new kid provided coverage in order for her to escape. Like a military combatant, the rookie lay down ground fire. Regrettably though, just before the rookie gave the all-clear sign, Jack asked him a question.

"So, are you sure it's a nineteen seventy bug?" the owner probed. "I'd hate to sell you the wrong parts."

"Yes sir, I'm sure."

"Alright then, I'm almost done." Boasting a little more about his vehicle, he continued, "Do you know that my car has a swivel sun visor? It also has automatic windshield wipers. Man, my vehicle is still the top of the line.

Distracted, the teenager replied, "That is great."
Glancing over to Raven, he was finally able to give the sign.
Timing the getaway perfectly, he launched both hands over his
head in the shape of the letter 'X'. When his arms came back
down, the traceuse bolted.

"I'm out of here," Rave whispered to herself. Then,
clearing the gate, she crossed the road and vanished.

Throughout the entire ordeal, while the rookie attempted a
rescue mission, the rest of the X sat silently inside Luke's car in
stealth mode. Parking directly across from Jack's Junkyard, the
team watched the event transpire. Upon spotting Raven, Rocco
opened the back passenger door and pulled her inside.

"Where have you been?" Luke pried.

While she debriefed, Solen still stood inside Jack's office.
Unfortunately, for him, Jack hadn't given up on his new
customer. "That will be two hundred and seventy-four dollars!"
he calculated. If I pull the parts for you, add another twenty-five
bucks."

"Oh shoot!" the teen grappled. "Sir, I didn't realize how
expensive parts could be. I can't afford to pay that much money.
I'll have to think about it and come back next week."

Ready to bargain, the owner suggested, "Well, how about
making it only two hundred dollars and I'll pull the parts for
free?"

"Sir, once again, I do appreciate all the time you spent.

I'm sorry, but I don't have that kind of money. Thank you for your help," the teenager concluded.

While the proprietor stood disappointed, Solen walked out the front door of the office building. Upon hitting the street, he darted toward Luke's vehicle. As soon as he got to the car, Jack spotted the automobile.

Realizing he had been bamboozled, he shouted, "Darn kids!" Hollering again, he added, "I've been punk'd!'

Like an agitated hornet, Jack Johnson fumbled out his front door unto the sidewalk. Raging mad, he hobbled toward the vehicle. Spotting him approaching, Luke stomped on the vehicle's gas pedal and accelerated down the road.

While they dashed, Jack leaped up and down, hurling insults in their direction. "And don't you ever come back here again!" he concluded. With nothing further to do, the business owner went inside his office.

"Dude, what the heck were you two thinking?" Luke shouted. Directing his anger toward Raven, he blasted, "Didn't you get the call?"

"Yeah, I got it," she admitted.

"We got it," the rookie interjected.

"Why didn't you get out?" the guru questioned.

"Well, I froze," the traceuse divulged.

"You did what?" the X leader hollered.

"I got scared," she confessed.

"Scared?" Luke seemed astonished.

"I'm not sure what happened," Solen further clarified, "but we both took off for the gate together. When I turned around, Raven was gone. The only option for me was to save her."

"Dude, it was sick!" Rocco interrupted. "You were in there a long time, bro. We saw everything and thought you were toast!"

"That's crazy insane, bro," Slim added. "You were a goner."

"It was kind of scary," the rookie acknowledged.

Easing the tension, Gordon teased, "You had Jack under an optical illusion, kid. You even pulled off an undercover operation!"

"Honestly, I didn't know if it would work," the rookie admitted.

"Thanks for looking out for me," the queen approved. "I had you all wrong from the start. You're alright, kid," she declared.

"I'd do it again for any X member!" the recruit boasted. Then, in self-reproof, he confessed, "Well, actually, it's my fault, too."

"Go on," Luke inquired.

"Well, along our trek, as Raven and I traveled the path, I lost focus."

"What happened?" Gordon inquired.

"I wiped out," the rookie admitted.

"The speed master wrecked, bro!" Rocco taunted.

"Yeah, I ate the dirt," he replied. "While checking some wall graffiti, I missed my mark and tripped over a large metal container. The wicked spill gashed me." Lifting his leg, he stated, "Here, check it out."

"Ouch!" Slim grimaced.

"Did it hurt?" Gordon inquired.

"No, actually, my pride got banged up more than my body. Getting up from the crash, I felt sorry for myself. Wanting to document the moment, I used my phone to snap photos. While taking pictures of the wall markings, I spotted an unusual symbol. After photographing it, I also took a pic of my leg. I sent all the photos to everyone," he confessed.

Hastily reaching for her cell phone, Raven clicked on her phone's inbox, opening the attachments. After viewing the pics, she passed the electronic device around. While it circulated, Rocco pressed the rookie further.

"You obviously heard the bad code, right?" he inquired

"Sure, I heard it," Sol responded. "Right when *creeper* was called, I found Raven. Together we jetted back to the front gate."

After the recruit's retort, Luke decided to squash any negativity. "Although the X ran into a few problems today, overall everything turned out well. For our next jam, if *creeper* is called, get out right away. We are all very lucky that nobody got caught." With one last proclamation he shouted, "X never die!"

Hooting aloud, Gordon added, "The junkyard rocked!"

"Bet!" Slim Jim agreed.

"It's a jamming time!" Rocco whooped.

"For sure," the traceuse approved.

"Rave and I hit insane vaults!" the new kid declared. "We rocked the site!"

"Yeah, I'm glad that everyone had a great time," Luke concluded. "The junkyard isn't for a weak athlete."

As soon as the team's guru finished speaking, Solen asked, "Can you identify all of the photos for me?"

Grabbing the phone, Slim replied, "Well, that's Westwood. They throw down their sign all over. Don't you see the W?"

Snatching the wireless device, Luke scrolled to another picture. "That marking is Funk! They use the Old English alphabet. It's someone's street name." Keeping the phone, he then scrolled to the unusual symbol. Baffled by it, he responded, "I should know that one but I don't."

"Show it to Gordon," Raven insisted. "He can translate anything."

"Hello!" Gordon proclaimed. "That is not a street sign. That's the symbol triquetrous. It's a three-cornered shape that's connected at every side with three interior angles. It isn't a typical triangle. A triquetrous can represent three units. It was used in Germanic paganism, Celtic polytheism, and even Christianity. It is a universal sign bringing together three separate but equal partners. Triquetrous can represent either good or evil. It all depends upon the host and your interpretation."

"Did you say 'host'?" Rocco interrupted.

"Yes, it all depends on who it is representing. Although, finding it in a junkyard could be either a warning or bad sign," the G confessed.

"What kind of warning?" Raven questioned. "What kind of bad sign?"

"I don't know," he replied. "Maybe three different crews are merging as one?"

"Man, no way!" Luke rebutted. "That doesn't happen on the street. A crew doesn't unite with another."

"Well, then what does it mean?" Slim pried.

"I'm not sure, but we'll probably find out soon," assured the G-man.

When he concluded, the team returned to talking about the day's successful flow. Except for a few slight mishaps, the X had conquered da' bomb.

As an alternative to splitting up, Luke proposed, "Let's cruise to my crib. We can hang there."

Chapter 7
The Westside

After zooming through the neighborhood that Saturday afternoon, the X spent a few hours chilling in Luke's swimming pool. Turning on his wireless device, the guru cranked up music for his guests. The tunes echoed the latest melody. Kicking things up a notch, Luke also offered food and beverages to his friends.

"Hey, the yard is a sweet flow," Gordon admitted. "There are a few possible snags out there, but overall it's fun."

"Right on!" Slim agreed. "I enjoyed it today. You should have seen the rock star and me ripping on the carrier," he boasted.

"Man, we blazed!" Rocco hollered. "We pulled off stellar moves," he added.

"Hey, we shredded it up too," Raven said. "Sol and I hit a nice trail with sick vaults!"

"Yeah, we blasted through the yard. Well, at least up until the point I crashed," the rookie confessed.

Poking fun at him, Rocco replied, "I still can't believe you wrecked. That's hilarious, bro!"

"Well, it is a stupid mistake," the recruit admitted.

"Don't worry about it, kid," Luke threw in. "That can happen to anyone."

"Yeah, I guess so," Sol replied.

"Hey, by the way," Luke added, "the G-man and I

completed insane cat leaps!"

"True, amen to that," Gordon praised. "We soared!"

The X acknowledged that the site had similar characteristics to an advanced level course. They knew that an inexperienced athlete could easily become distracted by the yard's complexity. With such a difficult gig, things could go wrong. A site labeled da' bomb provided a vast array of extremely complex obstacles. If not geared up, a traceur or traceuse would get crushed. Preparation was the key to success.

"If you fail to plan, you better plan to fail," the X leader reiterated. "It's our team motto."

While Luke's comrades took advantage of an aquatic occasion, Luke began to daydream. Memories from his past flashed from his hippocampus cortex.

Sadly, when Luke was two, his dad divorced his mother. Raising him alone, mom had all the parental duties of two people. As Luke grew, he could have made life easier for her, but he didn't. As a child, his skill set superseded that of his peers, and as a natural born athlete, he stood up to any challenge. His daring antics even earned him the name "dare devil" from his childhood acquaintances.

Upon reaching his teenage years, Luke discovered parkour. When he did, it became a gigantic part of his life. By creating fluid movement, Luke unleashed his inner emotions in outward creativity. Unbeknown to others, Luke's anger perpetuated every maneuver. With rage, his athletic performances would transform into extreme feats.

Luke's anger was nothing new, even if the expression of it was. In childhood, Luke became irate while attempting to go through life without a father. For years, he harbored anger, but, not wanting to endure the pain any longer, he hoped for a positive change. After voluntarily enrolling in a big brother mentor program, Luke's mom finally saw a difference.

At a local ministry, a weekly meeting offered teenagers a chance to interact with older helpful role models. At first, things didn't go so well. The X leader didn't discuss his personal issues. Shutting down became a weekly occurrence. After a few months, though, things started to transform. Recalling his mother's sentiment, she alleged, "A huge transformation transpired that year."

Before Luke ever requested help, his depression became unbearable. It stemmed from anger directly correlated to living his life without a dad. After being mentored by a positive adult role model though, *truth* relieved his anger by allowing him to move forward with his life. As soon as he forgave his father, the burden shifted. Although unable to fix the past, Luke Bail's pain was gone.

With a sigh of relief and one final glance back, the senior captain offered a proposition to his crew. "Hey, there's a freestyle breaker dance going on at three o'clock today. It's down on Third Street. The winner takes home a cash prize. We need to be there!"

"I'm there, bro!" Slim shouted. "It will be off the chain!"

"Let's do it!" Rocco hooted.

Hyped for a good time, the X hit the street. Even walking, they arrived at the boogie scene within twenty minutes. As the troupe descended upon the event, the live band reverberated with hot lyrics.

"Block party!" Raven hollered.

The booming music combined modern mixed groove and classic hip-hop. The unplugged street celebration turned into a reveling jam. A local disc jockey spun old school records while vendors sold fresh gear and souvenirs.

Talking over the music, Gordon yelled, "*Yo*, this place is *phat*!"

"It's where it's at!" Solen agreed.

"Bet!" Slim reiterated. "But, where's the dance contest?" he questioned.

Spotting it, Luke replied, "Looks like they're getting down over there," he pointed. "Let's check it out!"

Immediately, the X darted toward the dance floor. Getting stopped at the sign-in booth, the event's coordinator, wearing a nametag that read "Jazz," requested that they sign in.

"This here is a freestyle showdown!" he told them. "You can enter as a team or dance alone."

"Can we do both?" Luke inquired.

"That's fine," he replied. "But first, let's see a team performance and then run solo," Jazz replied.

"What time do we dance?" Raven inquired.

"If your crew wants to participate, you're up next," he suggested.

Just then, as Jazz finished speaking, the rhythmic composition changed pace. The music turned breaker style.

"Let's do it, peeps!" Luke shouted.

Lining up quickly on stage, the X stood in a single row across the dance floor. Like clockwork, in slow motion each member imitated the next. Attempting to keep up, the rookie mirrored their breaker motion. By following along, Solen maintained his composure.

"It's robotic!" a girl shouted from the crowd.

After a few minutes of a flawless performance, the music abruptly changed tempo, speeding up the beat. Adjusting to the rhythm, team X unleashed their potential, turning the dance into individualized interpretation.

Performing solo stunts, each member entertained the audience by adding unique technically insane maneuvers. Desiring to bring the group effort to a whole new level, Raven took center stage. Utilizing her gymnastic skill, she went airborne. After adding a killer front and back flip, her sidewinder helicopter brought the house down.

"Rip it up, rip it up, rip it up," the crowd chanted.

It was obvious to everyone that the X had stolen first place in the contest.

"They are the best!" a delirious audience member

shouted.

Ironically, just after the spectator shouted her approval, Rocco overstepped the stage's platform and clipped another spectator on the chin. After falling to the ground, the guy got back onto his feet.

"Punk!" he shouted. "That's disrespect! Sucker, you crossed me!" The kid jeered. Getting into Rocco's face, he threatened, "The *W* is in the house!"

"Oh man, my bad, bro!" the Roc apologized. "We're straight, right?"

Trying to fix the messy situation, the entire X team stepped forward attempting to make amends.

"It's too late!" another gang affiliate yelled.

In the blink of an eye, the dance competition went south. It turned from festive groove to street brawl. Knowing that "W" meant "Westside," the X squad became guarded. Being thirty strong, the Westside outnumbered Luke's crew five to one. Turning from bad to worse, a large cluster of thugs rolled up and gathered at center stage.

In an attempt to squash the inevitable skirmish, Jazz shouted on the microphone, "Work it out, ya'll. We don't want any trouble out here today. Why don't you dance for it?"

From across the room, the leader of the Westside shouted, "Nope, it's on!"

With that comment, Luke immediately pulled up his squad. While darting from off the dance floor into the street, he yelled, "Jet!" Directing his friends toward safety, he continued, "Split into teams of two!"

Instantly, Rocco grabbed Raven and Gordon pulled Slim with him. Watching the group disperse, the X leader snagged Solen by the shirt. To the rookie's disbelief, Luke pulled him in the opposite direction—*toward* Westwood territory.

"Where are you going?" the recruit bellowed. "Are you crazy, bro?"

"Just keep up," the veteran replied. In no time, Luke had brought Solen across the municipality into unfamiliar terrain.

Glancing behind, the rookie shouted, "They're still coming!"

"Keep moving kid," the guru persuaded.

Knowing that the W wanted him eliminated on their own home turf, Luke's mission became survival.

"They're about fifteen deep," the rookie shouted to his boss. "What's the plan?"

Turning around, Luke grabbed Sol and shoved him into a rundown commercial building.

"Go inside," he yelled.

By taking the caboose, the guru shielded the novice from harm. Entering through the front door of the vacant structure, Solen blast into the main lobby with his mentor close behind. Within seconds, the youth zoomed back outside using a rear exit. After stumbling upon the backside of the lot, the traceurs raced onward.

Turning around once again, the rookie updated, "They're only fifty yards away!"

Spotting a five-story vacant facility, Luke shouted, "Head that way, kid!"

He knew, if completely unoccupied, the building was ideal for a disappearing act. Furthermore, he recalled that most empty buildings still offered an array of left-behind furniture. It created an obstacle course for an athlete.

Taking the lead once again, Luke yelled, "We're going inside, bro! Gotta get off the street!"

Hoping to flee from the enemy, the rookie agreed, "Okay, it's worth a shot!"

Up until that point, it had been a sprint for their lives experience. Upon reaching the facility, in full stride, Luke completed a thief vault, leaping through a windowless casing. By transferring his bodyweight, he entered the five-story complex. Then, by jetting forward toward the stairwell, he blast across the first floor. Shadowing him, Solen completed the same trek.

"Keep moving, kid!" Luke reminded.

In the meantime, while the X leader and his recruit cleared danger, Rocco and Raven had their hands full as well. They were now in a corner, where the Westside had chased them into a back alley, trapping them inside.

While confronting six punks, Rocco shouted to Raven, "Get behind me!" Pulling her backward, he threatened the W, "It's time to *throw down!*"

As he spoke, one Westside member charged at him. Without hesitation, the ironman blocked the assault and forced the assailant into a wall. The impact knocked the aggressor out cold. Observing the incident, the other five thugs became furious. Within seconds, they surrounded Raven and Rocco. Taking cheap shots, each affiliate randomly fired punches in Roc's direction.

Fortunately for him, he blocked every blow. Attempting to help out, Raven also kept the attackers at bay utilizing a power leg thrust. After an intense barrage of firepower from the Westside, the situation intensified.

"Bring it on!" the strongman encouraged. "Show me what you got!"

In a desperate move, Rocco taunted his attackers. Although slightly perplexed by that tactic, the Westside stepped forward desiring to finish off the two X members.

Unbeknown to the enemy though, Rocco's skill set was superior. As high school state wrestling champ, he had gone undefeated at forty-four and zero that year. Known as "the beast" to his friends, he never backed down from a formidable challenge.

"Game on!" Roc shouted once more.

His comment put a grin on Raven's face. Getting into a ready stance, she shouted *"Kiai!"*

With the odds reversing in Rocs and Raven's favor, good overcame evil. Dismantling the hooligans, Rocco's bombardment of uppercuts and cross jabs sent the gang into a tailspin.

Providing backup, Raven unleashed her downward karate knife-chop. With raw strength and pure talent, the two X members jacked up the Westside boys. Stumbling from the back alley in defeat, the thugs attempted to gather the last of their dignity. In a monumental loss, they retreated.

"Where are you going?" Rocco hollered. "We're just getting started!"

As soon as the gang dispersed, Raven and Rocco decided to spurt toward home base. After winning the battle, they transitioned back into ordinary friendly citizens.

"Let's get going," the traceuse urged.

"Right on," Rocco agreed.

While they blasted in the direction of Luke's house, Gordon and Slim ran for their own safety.

Racing down a side street, Jim shouted, "They're still coming!"

Just as a predator pursues its prey, the Westside hunted.

Needing a good plan, Gordon finally spotted an opportunity. Pointing toward an open door, he hollered, "In there!"

Without flinching, the G-man led his pal into the unknown business to discover an industrial Laundromat housed in a warehouse–like building. After slipping inside, and locking the door behind them, the youths heading into the heart of a work facility. Quickly searching for a way out of the building, they avoided human contact by dodging through equipment. Moving aggressively, both Gordon and Slim flowed in the direction of the store's front office. Upon reaching it, they darted past the counter, out the entranceway, and into the street. Gordon knew that if Westside had seen them enter at all, they wouldn't expect them to have made it out a different exit so quickly. They had escaped.

"Let's get out of here!" Jim squealed.

"Head toward home," Gordon directed.

"Nice call," Slim praised. "The building idea worked out great."

"We really didn't have another option," G admitted.

Upon arriving at Luke's house, Raven greeted them asking, "Where's the boss?"

"We haven't seen him," Jim replied.

"What?" Rocco probed. "Weren't you with him?"

"No bro," the G-man denied. "We haven't seen him since the dance contest."

"Oh no, this is bad," Rocco said with a tremble. "We need to go search for him right away!"

"I hope the rookie is with him," Raven added with a grimace. "Let's take my truck. We'll find them!"

The vehicle's tires' screeched all the way down the road. Upon hitting the main highway, the team searched for their X leader and the rookie.

Meanwhile, as Raven and her pals drove into the city, the Westside continued stalking the X captain and his recruit.

Although the enemy advanced, both practitioners cleared obstacles inside the vacant building in order to avoid a beat down. By flowing over and around objects, Luke and Sol put space between them and their adversaries. In a last-ditch effort to get away, the teens darted up the stairwell. Luke led Solen onward until he reached the third level.

"This is *creeper*, bro!" he shouted to the novice. "Show me *what you got*!

Upon reaching the third story, Sol shouted back, "Dude, this level is sinister."

The hallway had an unearthly appearance; trash and garbage had piled up everywhere. An explosion of strangely familiar graffiti extended across the four walls. Each sign and symbol made a different proclamation, but, blotting out their competition, the Westside superimposed their "W" on top of all their opponents in a grand declaration of power.

"This is bad!" Solen clamored. "We shouldn't be here."

"Just keep moving," Luke countered.

"Get those punks!" a W member shouted.

"This is our turf!" another yelled.

"Spurt, bro!" Luke ordered Sol. "Keep running, man!"

Realizing he was getting sidetracked as he had in the junkyard, Sol started moving again. Just as he did, he spotted the sign of the triquetrous.

Chapter 8
Triquetr⬧us

"Keep flowing, bro!" Luke insisted.

"I'm on it," Sol reassured him.

Grabbing the rookie's arm, Luke placed the novice into the lead once again. "Follow the stairway to the fifth floor!"

Immediately dashing up the stairwell, Solen reached the fourth level.

"Go to the fifth!" the guru reminded.

The Westside still trailed team X desiring to hand them a street whooping. Persuading the new kid to move a little faster, Luke hollered, "Put on the jets, kid!"

Bouncing skyward, the teens completed a waist-high reverse vault over the aluminum alloy guardrail on the midway turn of the fourth story stairwell, which propelled them upward to the last set of stairs. Still searching for an escape route, the X captain spotted the fifth level access entry.

"Go through that door!" Luke bellowed.

"Bet!" the novice promised.

Upon reaching the entrance, Solen entered the room, swinging the door inward. He and Luke then dove inside an unoccupied hallway. After tumbling to the ground and bouncing back to their feet, Luke locked the fifth-level entry door. What they didn't know was that at that exact moment, the Westside stopped the pursuit. The thugs had stopped dead in their tracks as if they were seeing a ghost. Still uninformed that the chase had ended, Solen raced toward an adjacent room. For about five seconds, the rookie sped along with Luke trailing closely behind. Finally realizing that something had changed, the X captain persuaded his pal to stop.

Coming to a standstill, Luke claimed, "Something isn't right."

Solen, catching on, asked, "Where are they?"

Slowing slipping through the corridor, the teens suspected something sinister.

"They're setting us up!" Luke whispered.

"Oh man, this isn't good," the rookie answered, quivering. "Why aren't we being chased anymore?"

"I don't know, bro, but something is strange," his mentor replied.

"Is it a hoax?"

"This is definitively messed up," Luke assured.

Sunlight faintly illuminated the unoccupied office from a skylight above, providing just enough radiance to expose objects in close proximity. Standing in the faint glow, the teens discussed three possible escape routes.

"Dude, let's be safe," Luke counseled. "We need to move the furniture and block each entry. If the Westside push through one door, we will move the furniture and run out a different route.

"Sounds good to me," agreed the rookie.

They first slid a large couch in front of the fifth-level access door. Then they pulled a love seat toward a security exit fire escape. Finally, blocking a tan partition slider, they pushed a large black executive desk into position, separating one room from another.

"Everything's in position, captain," Sol stated. "What do we do now, bro?"

"Since the Westside can come through any one of those entries, even simultaneously, maybe would should find a *fourth* option for a way out of here?" Luke insisted. "Let's look around, but be on your guard."

Walking around the facility, the teens brainstormed. In cautious optimism, they discussed various possibilities.

The novice proposed, "What about a window?"

"Whoa dude, we're on the fifth floor bro!" Luke reminded.

"Come on man, it's worth a shot."

"Alright then, let's go with that idea," his mentor approved.

They both knew that jumping five stories to the concrete below would be worse than a butt kicking from the Westside.

"We'll need a connection linking us to the ground," Sol pointed out.

"True," the leader agreed.

Without an alternative, Luke chose the third window. Peering outside, he brightened up. "We'll flow the *Cocos nucifera*!"

"What?" Solen asked, confused.

"Dude, we'll scale the palm tree!" Luke simplified.

"Spot on, chum, it's a perfect idea," the novice approved.

"Although extremely dangerous, I think it's a good plan," the guru insisted. "That palm is strong and narrow. We can grab it more easily. Its awkward shape will help us flow to the ground. It's even at an ideal angle—a one-hundred-degree half-moon arc."

"That sounds good to me," Solen approved.

"It's perfect!!" the X leader exulted.

With a premier athletic departure course established, the teens decided to conduct an exploration of the facility. Scampering around the room, they investigated a nearby corridor. Within a short distance, the traceurs came upon a conference area.

"There's office furniture inside here," the recruit assessed. "It looks like someone has been using it."

At first glance, the workplace's scenery appeared normal and sophisticated. On closer inspection, though, the boys noticed something odd. An iconic inscription had been chiseled into the chamber's plaster wall.

"That's intriguing," Solen said, indicating the engraving with his finger.

Instead of street tags and gang signs, the markings were clearly organized encryptions and ideograms—a code.

"Check it out, bro!" Luke pointed. "What are those?"

Joining Luke in front of the panel, Solen observed a pictorial resemblance of a physical object like something out of a history textbook regarding Egyptian culture.

After he examined it, Luke noted, "Each section looks like it was handcrafted with a simple chisel and impressed into the plasterboard."

The artwork was showcased over and over again across all four walls of the room.

"There are six pictures," the novice counted. "What do they mean?"

"I'm not sure, bro," Luke confessed. "But, I'll capture them on my phone."

Pulling out his electronic device, the guru carefully documented the six cryptograms and examined the photos to make sure they'd come through.

"*I've got it!*" he announced triumphantly.

Just then, the slider partition door opened and three older gentlemen stood in plain view.

"Whoa, dude!" the rookie screamed. "*Run!*"

Startled by the teen commotion, the men stumbled over each other trying to enter the office.

"*Chtó ti délayesh?*" a Russian voice yelled. "*What'z arez you'z doing? Yous gets out ofv thez place!*" the man shouted.

"Oh snap!" the X leader shrieked. "It's time to jet, kid!"

While sliding his phone into a front pocket, Luke pulled

the recruit by his shirt toward the third window. Upon reaching it, the guru shouted, "You jump first, rookie!"

Without hesitation, Solen cat leaped over the windowsill and, while in midair, reached for the palm. Grabbing the tree, he wrapped his arms around its trunk. His fierce speed propelled his body outward upon contact, rotating his legs wide. While spinning around the shaft, Sol pushed off the tree's trunk. Twisting skyward back to center, his feet landed directly on top of the waxy bark. Utilizing every ounce of agility and concentration he had, the rookie balanced himself while standing fifty feet above the ground.

"I hope this works!" he shouted over to his mentor. Sol extended and locked his front leg at a thirty degree angle, letting his back leg provide support and help him maintain his posture. Rapidly sliding, the recruit blasted toward earth like a missile. With both arms spread wide, he balanced surfer style as he raced toward the ground. *Cowabunga!*" he shouted.

When he was ten feet from the ground, Solen completed a double front flip just before striking the tree's arching half-moon end point. Converting the maneuver into a tuck roll, he landed safely on the dirt below.

Luke, watching from the window, called down, "You're insane, bro!"

Being time for his escape, the X leader took one final glimpse back at the three imposing men who were now swiftly approaching the window. He made a mental note of their appearance. He knew the first was Russian from his speech. The second was stocky and looked Irish. The third was clearly of African descent but had eerie yellow eyes.

Utilizing a screwdriver to Kong vault, Luke leaped over the windowsill, grabbing the tree. After wrapping his arms around the trunk, his momentum brought both legs back to center. While hanging underneath, he linked his fingers together and fastening his legs around its trunk.

"Whoa, I'm out of here!" Luke hollered.

The guru navigated downward using a firefighter pole slide to the ground. Luke's visual perspective differed from Solen's. Fortunately for him, by digging his heals into the tree's bark, he stopped right in front of the trunk's half-moon arc. When he did, without faltering, the X leader released his arm grip so that his entire body dangled upside down by his feet.

Grinning at his buddy below, he hollered, "Do you double dare me to let go?"

"Come on you slow possum," Sol snickered. "We need to get moving."

After releasing his leg grip, Luke performed a backward tuck summersault with both arms spread eagle. Landing on the ground, he promptly threw his hands above his head like a gymnast.

"It's a ten!" the novice announced.

"Thank you very much," Luke concurred. "Now, it's time to surge!"

The teens ran from the vacant lot, but they clearly heard the Russian man hollering from above, "*Youz boyz stay outz of herez*, and *dontz comez back!*"

Vanishing in a jiffy, both Luke and Sol transitioned into the street. Upon hitting the main road, the rookie asked, "What happened back there?"

"That's real gangsters, kid," Luke said. "Now, let's get out of Westside territory."

Within moments, after turning down a dirt road, the X leader spotted a red truck. Sprinting in that direction, he shouted, "It's Raven!"

"We're rescued!" the rookie hooted.

The truck came to a stop, and the front passenger door popped open. Jumping out, Rocco asked, "Did someone call for a taxi?"

Giving him dap, the Luke replied, "Dude, it's great to see you, man!"

"Hop in," Gordon said, motioning from inside the truck. "Let's roll!"

In a jiffy, the X zoomed away from Westside terrain. Back together, the crew ecstatically conversed about that day's affair. Before getting out of the vehicle that afternoon, Luke reminded everyone about Sunday's event, saying, "Chung's at eight o'clock."

Chapter 9
Chung Fu

Arriving fifteen minutes early on Sunday morning, Luke stood outside Chung Fu. As a weekly ritual, the X leader trained at the facility. While standing there waiting alone, he announced to himself, it's time to educate the rookie. Not being able to sleep very well the night before, Luke wrestled with the events that had occurred on Saturday. That day had been unforgettable. During their X venture, the crew managed to jam at the junkyard, rip it up at the dance contest, and survive an attempted beat down from the Westside.

"Man, yesterday was hostile," the guru said out loud. Recalling the confrontation with the three men, Luke added, "Thank God we made it out!"

Spooked by the nightmarish affair, neither he nor the recruit had told the other members about the encounter. Not ready to discuss what had happened, the X leader and the rookie had made a pact. Hoping Sol kept his mouth shut, he grumbled, "That new kid better not say anything!"

While he sat replaying the episode, Dan, the owner of Chung Fu, unlocked the gate and lifted the bay door. Inviting his first patron inside, Dan greeted Luke warmly. "Hey, buddy, how are you this morning?"

"I'm great!" Luke replied. "The rest of the crew will be here soon," he added.

"Okay, good. How many members are working out today?" Dan inquired.

"We have six members now," Luke stated proudly.

"Excellent! Are they all coming?" Dan asked.

"Yes sir!" the X leader guaranteed.

"Alright then, the price is ten bucks per person for three hours. So, it will be sixty bucks total for your group today."

"That's fine," Luke answered.

Changing his mind, Dan threw in, "Um, well, just pay me fifty dollars and you can have the entire gym until noon. I don't expect to get any other business this morning," he added.

"Awesome! I'll get the money right away," Luke promised. Walking back outside, he spotted the rest of the X arriving. With everyone chipping in money, the team secured the facility.

"Time to train, peeps! We have exclusive access until noon!" Luke boasted.

"Sweet!" Slim yelped. "Let's hit the floor!"

After paying Dan, the squad warmed up and stretched. Rocco informed the new kid about the ways of Chung Fu. "This is gnarly place, man! You have to be invited here in order to train at this site."

"That's cool," Solen responded.

"Just wait until you see how Dan has this place tricked out!"

With the floor protected by padding, the gym encouraged bigger and higher stunts.

"Who is the new kid?" the proprietor questioned.

"Hi, I'm Solen," the recruit replied. You have a nice gym."

"I appreciate the compliment," Dan replied, shaking Sol's hand.

Raven pleaded, "Mr. Dan, can you please school the newbie in the way of Fu?"

"No problem," he replied. Turning toward Sol the owner asked, "Are you ready?"

"Please tell!" the recruit begged.

With captivating energy, Dan shouted, "The name "Chung Fu" is derived from communication and cooperation. It's a way of life. It's about having a deep impact on other people. As an inspirational leader, first you get to know a person. Always be honest and sincere, and go beyond a surface level partnership."

"What do you mean?" Solen inquired.

"In order for someone to trust you, you must believe in them. Belief will blossom when prejudice is set aside."

"But, I don't look down on anyone," the draftee assured.

"That is good," Dan acknowledged. "But Fu also applies to your team members. You are a group of parkour athletes."

"But, technically it's an individual sport," Solen insisted.

"I understand that," the owner agreed. "But you are one squad. There should be a partnership among associates. Chung

Fu only works when there is a mutual agreement."

"Oh, I sort of understand," the rookie said with hesitation.

Seeing the confused look, Dan replied, "Well, let me clarify. The X has six members. Is that true?"

"Yes!" Solen assured him.

"No, you are wrong!" Dan countered. "You didn't hear me earlier. You are *one*!"

"Oh, I get it!" swore the recruit.

"Son, it's time for you to learn Fu!"

"Yes sir!"

"We will talk more next visit. Now, go out and enjoy the facility!"

Dispersing, the X entered the fitness center. With all the equipment at their disposal, the teens rattled the recreational site. With great attention to the development of physical and mental well-being, Dan had stocked the gym with apparatus designed especially for parkour.

Divided into three separate sections, the first room provided everything needed for plyometrics—a type of exercise created to bridge the gap between speed and strength. Its conventional hub helped a traceur and traceuse spring higher and leap further. Using a systematic sequence of small boxes and wall boards, an athlete could reach his or her peak physical state.

Unlike the first area, the second simulated an industrial playground. With all the rubber items, the possibilities were limitless. A practitioner could practice the dive, king, reverse, speed, thief, dash, or, even the mighty rocket vault without as much danger of injury.

The third room section was fashioned with a series of platforms and ropes. The section was set high above the rest of the gym to foster true muscular endurance. Encouraging midair acrobatic movement, the cross bars and hand rings hung fifteen feet above the floor. In order to provide maximum protection and support, the landlord placed a quadruple layer of padding on top of the floorboards.

"This joint is phat!" the rookie bellowed.

"True!" Slim replied.

"Alright, people, it's show time!" Luke hollered.

With Raven trailing behind, Rocco ran full blast into the third room. "Let's roll, chick!" he howled

"Let me see what you got!" she responded.

Darting directly to a towering aerial fortress, the team's strongman launched upward. Grabbing a platform with one hand, he lifted himself to center stage. Then, springing into action, he scaled a rope and shimmied across the course hand-over-hand. Upon hitting the track's midway point, he released his grasp, falling to earth. As soon as he landed on the padded floor, Raven pulled a similar stunt.

"Man, they are shredding it up!" Gordon boasted. "Let's hit the precision, kid!" he yelled to Slim.

"Bet!" the sly one replied.

Responding to the challenge, Jim completed a thief vault

over a five-foot-by-five foot foam square. Then Slim hit every tactical jump possible. As he did, Gordon conducted his own parkour interpretation. While they busted out in athletic expression, Luke and his recruit surged toward plyometrics.

"You're good," the X leader praised, "but this will make you better!"

"Show me how it's done, captain!" Solen teased.

Answering the dare, the instructional specialist led his trainee through a rigorous workout.

"Try to keep up, bro!" the mentor challenged.

"No problem!" the new kid bragged. "*Bring it!*"

Unleashing his mojo, Luke hit a climatic moment by blasting over a ten-foot wall. Turn vaulting over the top surface and facing reverse, he completed a *castaway bomb* by pushing off, flipping backward, and then landing on the floor below. His meticulous attention to detail showed. Turning things up a notch, the team's commander then combined a series of powerful maneuvers while charging across the facility. His succession of moves astounded the rookie. While Sol gasped for air, the guru pushed his recruit to the breaking point.

Taunting Solen, he shouted, "Where is your speed now, kid?"

Stunned, the rookie could only reply, "*Nice!*"

In rapid sequence, Luke attacked an arrangement of strategically positioned wall panels. Tacking between two narrow dividers, he became airborne, utilizing the walls' plastic support brackets. Leaping from left to right, Luke sprang through the air from one partition to the next. Without hesitation, the rookie shadowed his mentor at the same speed. When they reached the apex, both teens performed a wall dismount.

While Luke and Sol practiced airborne transitions, Jim and Gordon achieved vaulting mastery. After about twenty minutes, they finalized their circuit with Slim recommending a team water break.

"Let's take five, peeps!" he shouted to the crew.

After a rest, the teens agreed to swap stations and hit a second round of training. Within fluid movement, the X spent Sunday's sunrise at Chung Fu.

When the cardiovascular lesson ended, the teens took advantage of the gym's shower to freshen up before hitting the street so they wouldn't have to head straight home. Before walking out, they gave Dan a farewell.

"Hey, I'm glad you came to see me today," the owner stated. "Please don't forget that Chung Fu will be closed next weekend. I will be out of town," he added.

"Sure," Luke replied. "Then, we will see you the following Sunday," he assured him.

"Great!" Dan agreed. "Hey rookie, don't forget that Fu is about unity. You are one team."

"Yes sir," Sol replied. "I won't forget."

Gathering outside the fitness complex, the X departed.

"Does anyone want a smoothie?" Gordon asked. "Let's

go to Blenders. My girlfriend works there," he added.

"That is a great idea, bro," Slim agreed.

"Count me in," Raven said. "Jenna will definitely hook us up! If anyone needs a ride, we can take my truck," she offered.

"Let's go then," Rocco replied.

"Count me out," the rookie declined. "I have to hang with my family today."

"Count me out, too," Luke added. "I need to help my mom finish repairs on the house. She's been asking me for weeks. When I'm done, I'll catch up with everyone tonight. Oh yeah, by the way, don't forget that we have a Fusion meeting at Upward Assembly tonight at seven," he concluded.

"Ah man, I'm not sure about that," Rocco rebutted. "You guys can go. I'll probably just chill at home."

"Dude, it's free pizza night!" Slim insisted.

Raven joined in. "You can't pass up free pizza! Besides, it is only a thirty-minute gathering. After that, we play indoor soccer."

"True!" Gordon concurred.

Luke reminded his team, "You all know my history. I *need* to be there."

"You're right, man," Rocco apologized. "I'll go."

"Everyone is going!" Raven confirmed.

That being a done deal, the group split—Raven and her passengers drove for smoothies while the team leader and the recruit sped toward home.

Dropping Solen off at his house, Luke promised, "Hey bro, I'll pick you up tonight for Fusion. It's on the way and no big deal."

"Hey, that's cool," Sol approved. "I'll see you later."

While they called it a day, the traceuse and her voyagers enjoyed smoothies. "I'll be back to get everyone around six thirty," she pledged as she dropped each person off.

Chung Fu-

One!

Chapter 10
Fusion

That Sunday night, the X met at Fusion in order to attend the Upward event. Parking near the back door of the building, they gathered together in somber fashion.

Raven stated, "Today begins the last week of school."

"Thanks for reminding us," Gordon snarled.

"Oh yeah, I almost forgot that exams start this week," Slim grumbled.

"But graduation is next Saturday," Rocco pointed out cheerfully.

"You guys are killing me!" Raven hollered. "You're making it worse."

While graduation was something to look forward to, unfortunately it also meant that Fusion was ending.

"Although tonight will be our last session at Upward Assembly, everything will be fine," Luke said. "Besides, summer is just around the corner. We're still taking the trip to Europe," he guaranteed.

Piggybacking on the X leader's proclamation, Gordon hollered, "Don't forget that Copenhagen has the ultimate parkour park!"

"Hey, that's right!" the rookie approved. "We will be jamming!"

"Alright," Raven promised, "I won't whine anymore. I'm

sure that everything will be okay."

"I guarantee you that the X will never split up!" Luke vowed. "No matter what happens, we will always be together!"

"Yeah, preach it, captain!" Rocco commended.

"Hey," the guru said to change the mood, "I want to take a team picture!"

"You better make me copies," Raven threatened.

"Anything for you, darling," he teased.

"I'm only taking *one* pic," Rocco swore, "So get us all in the first time."

After Luke completed the photo shoot, which was way more than one picture, the X entered the youth center, where the instructor's assistant greeted them.

"Glad to see you made it out," he said with a smile.

"Did I miss the pizza?" Jim inquired.

"Zip it!" Raven rebuked pulling on Slim's ear. "Where's the respect?"

"Sorry about that, teacher-man," the sly one apologized.

"It's all good," the teacher replied. Then, turning to Luke, he greeted, "Good evening, bro! It's nice to see you again!"

"Likewise," the lead traceur assured him. "I'm glad to be here sir."

Since his conversion, Luke walked daily in his newfound hope. Though he was a transformed man only inwardly, everyone recognized the difference *outwardly*.

"Welcome back to Fusion," the general instructor said

while scanning the room. "I'm glad to see everyone here tonight. As you are aware, this is a very special evening. This will be our last Sunday together until August." After pausing, he continued. "Today, we will only spend ten minutes reviewing the Good Book. After that, we will play soccer and eat pizza." Gathering his notes, he began his lesson by saying, "Last week, we discussed *purpose*." Looking around the room, he questioned, "Did anyone take the time to reflect on that message?"

After a few teens raised their hands, the instructor continued. "Last Sunday we learned that there is a plan for your life. To further enlighten you, tonight we will talk about walking *in your purpose*. You may not realize it, but it's a daily responsibility." In excitement, the speaker added, "It is soul deep!" The minister talked on for a few more minutes and then switched into a question-and-response session. When that concluded, all participants dashed over to the mess hall for munchies. While eating, the preacher stood up and announced, "I just want to congratulate our seniors. They will be graduating this week. We are proud of them!" Before concluding he added, "I want to remind everyone once again that Upward will restart at the end of summer."

When the instructor finished speaking, he directed the teens to the indoor soccer floor. After a few games, the night came to an end. Departing from the complex, the X met outside in the rear parking lot, where they agreed to meet again on Thursday, the day after the last final exams.

"After we pass our exams," Raven proclaimed, "it'll be time for a new gig!

"Demark or bust!" the rookie declared

"We're going," Luke confirmed. "You better believe it!"

"Wahoo!" Slim Jim howled.

"We're there," the G-man guaranteed.

Snapping the squad back to reality, Raven prompted, "We have to start making plans. I can scout a local travel agency. Actually, my uncle works at Blitz Travel. He will find us a deal!"

"You go, girl!" the lead traceur cheered. "Get it done!"

After discussing their summer plans, each X member departed for home to study for the upcoming exams. As Monday morning rapidly approached, the sun dawned a new day.

That morning, while heading to first period, Raven shouted to Rocco, "Have fun taking your test!"

"Hey kid," he replied, "I can't wait until this is done."

"It will be over before you know it," the traceuse assured.

"Well, I'll catch you later."

While they went their separate ways, the rest of the X had already started testing. At the end of the day, when everyone was finished with exams there wasn't much to do.

Happily for Luke, his teacher had reserved the media center in the library. The instructor directed all of the students who'd finished their exams to the unoccupied computers.

"No inappropriate sites," the teacher reminded them.

While surfing the Internet, Luke reviewed a few local

articles concerning daily events. Getting bored, he then conducted another search. After checking an online sporting site, he gave up on his Web hunt; running out of things to do that didn't require downloading programs to the library computer.

Luke pulled out his cell phone despite the school rules against it and started flipping through the applications. Spooling over to the message center first, Luke didn't see any new e-mail. Then, scrolling over to the camera option, he spotted a button flashing. Pushing it, his most recent photos uploaded.

"Oh yeah, these are pics of the team," he whispered to himself. While navigating through the pictures, Luke had a mischievous idea. The team's mastermind decided to e-mail his crew the photos. Knowing that they were still taking their exams, he whispered, "This is the perfect occasion!" Chuckling he added, "I can only imagine their faces when their phones start buzzing. They never turn them off! *They're going to freak*!"

With a simple push, Luke completed his joke. Sending the snaps, he then fumbled through the phone's tool menu. When he did, things got interesting.

Accidentally hitting the wrong key on the keypad, the device skipped back to older images. Unbeknown to him, his phone was equipped with image recognition. The apparatus was able to compare images with information on the Web, finding matches and relevant pages.

"Oh shoot," Luke whispered, mistakenly activating the control panel. The phone lit up, reminding its operator that more images needed to be retrieved. The X leader opened the viewer and saw the six pictographs he'd documented earlier.

"What the heck?" Luke asked.

Instantly, six bizarre cryptograms appeared on the phone's screen. What was odder was that words also materialized with the symbols in sequential order. Next to each icon, a word or group of words flashed across the phone's interactive surface, referencing the hieroglyph.

"What is going on?" the guru asked in amazement.

Scrolling through, the translation flowed in order from right to left. By maneuvering his index finger over the screen, Luke activated a computerized voice, which read off, "◼ Triquetrous, ☐ by land, ⋈ by light, ☾ last waning moon, ⊞ Lascaux, and ✳ Christmas."

"*Holy mother of toast!*" Luke yelped. Looking up at the librarian, he retracted his comment saying, "My bad!"

Continuing with his personal business once again, he muttered, "This is ludicrous. I don't know what these symbols are, but I need to send them to the crew." Without thinking twice, Luke launched the electronic information to all X members. Instantaneously, during testing, five phones erupted again in musical melody. As this was the second time, Solen got busted. A song trumpeted throughout the classroom blasting a modern tune.

In disbelief, the instructor stood up and hollered, "Give me the phone, young man. Having it on is against testing policy.

"Yes sir, but I need it in case of an emergency," Sol

persuaded.

"I don't want your excuses," the examiner replied. "Bring me the phone. Then, hand in your test."

"Sir, please let me finish the exam. I'm really sorry!"

"Fine," the professor shouted, "Take your phone and test to the assistant principal's office. I'll call Mrs. Jones and let her know that you are coming.

Retrieving his exam and then walking out of the room, the rookie grumbled, "Oh man, I'm going to get a tail kicking."

After reaching the administrator's office, Mrs. Jones greeted Sol with disapproval. "What are you doing here?" she questioned. This is unlike you, Solen John Starr. You haven't had a referral all year. What is this about?"

"Well, I forgot to turn off my phone during testing," he admitted.

"That's unacceptable. You do understand the consequences for your actions, right? This incident can result in failing the exam and the overall course. You'll then have to take it again during summer school," the administrator clarified.

"Ma'am, I'm really sorry," Solen apologized.

"Please give me the phone," Mrs. Jones prompted. Reviewing the device, she stated, "It looks like someone sent you an e-mail attachment." Seeing the message flashing, she continued, "May I open it?"

Without stopping, the supervisor continued her investigation. After she opened the newly sent post, the symbolic icons lit up. The six-picture lithograph appeared on the screen, and next to each image a corresponding word or phrase appeared.

Baffled, she Mrs. Jones asked, "What is this?"

"I don't know." the senior replied. "Let me see it." After he took a glance, Solen stammered, "Um, well actually, my friend and I found some strange writing on a wall. Yeah, we were hanging out downtown," he explained.

"Keep talking," replied Mrs. Jones.

"Well, we found these weird signs while trekking. During a jam, we scanned the images to a phone," Solen said.

"That's an interesting story," the assistant principal granted. "So, let me get this straight. You found these symbols in at least one building downtown. Did you find any on this campus?

"Yes, we found the symbols. No, we didn't find them on campus," Sol clarified.

"Alright then, please take a seat out in the hallway. I'll be back in a few minutes."

The senior classman left the administrative chamber followed by Mrs. Jones. While Solen took a seat, Mrs. Jones proceeded down the hall to the office of the school's resident police officer. Going inside, she shut the door.

"Oh shoot, this is getting bad," the rookie muttered.

After about ten minutes, the assistant principal came back into the hallway accompanied by Mr. Walker. "Young man, please come with me," the officer requested.

Chapter 11
Investigate

That Monday afternoon, Solen found himself in the midst of an investigation. The professional staff hurled questions in his direction until he felt caught in a whirlwind. Although the senior answered each one, the administrators relentlessly interrogated him. He lost track of how many times he said, "Yes, we found the symbols around the city. No, we didn't find them here."

Pausing for a moment, the police officer then said, "You said *we*. Who else is involved?"

"Luke Bail. We were together when we found the symbols. Actually, he used his phone to scan them."

"Where is he right now? the deputy questioned.

"He is in class taking a test," Sol assured.

Turning to Mrs. Jones, the investigator requested, "Please call Luke to the office."

"I'm on it," she replied.

Within no time, Luke entered the room and the officer directed him to take a seat.

"Luke Bail, I presume?" the officer inquired. "I have a question for you, son. Are you the one that took the pictures of these symbols?"

"Yes," the X leader replied.

"Where were you?"

"We were in a building downtown."

"What were you doing there?" Mrs. Jones questioned.

"We were being chased," confessed the rookie.

With that response, Mrs. Jones rolled her eyes. "Great ..." she grumbled. "Solen, you didn't tell me *that* part. What is going on?"

Taking charge of the conversation once again, the police officer inquired, "Who chased you?"

Luke responded, "I will have to backtrack a little. First, we were at a dance contest. It was this past Saturday. For a while, things were going well. Then, it got ugly. Accidently overstepping our bounds, one of our team members messed up. When he did, a showdown ensued with a rival crew."

"So you're a gang?" The officer asked in a neutral tone.

"No sir," the X captain replied. "We consider ourselves organized athletic street performers."

"What do you mean?" Mrs. Jones asked.

Seizing the opportunity, Solen answered, "We enjoy parkour!"

"Go on," she requested.

"We have six members," he quantified. "As athletes, we select the most efficient way to overcome an obstacle by maneuvering through the environment."

"*Really*?" the officer probed. "Well, what about the rival crew? Are they a gang?"

"Yes!" Luke interrupted. "They are the Westside boys."

"Oh, I'm pretty familiar with that group," the policeman

admitted. "So, what happened?"

"The Westside chased us through the downtown area. We ran for cover inside a vacant building. While in there, we managed to make it to the top floor. On the fifth level, we found that weird writing on a wall. Being curious, I decided to scan the symbols to my phone," Luke concluded.

"Then, what happened?" Mrs. Jones inquired.

"Then, something even stranger occurred," Solen said with a shudder. "We ran into three men. They were *freaky*!"

"Alright, that's enough, this is getting way out of hand," the assistant principal interrupted. "We adults need to talk. You two boys go outside."

While in the lobby, both Luke and Solen sat dismayed.

"You started all of this. You sent the e-mail, bro!" the rookie complained.

"I know," the X leader admitted.

While the teens sat inside the reception area, the administrative team seemed to be having a debate. Occasionally, Mrs. Jones came outside, asked a few questions, and then left again. After what felt like forever, the adults called the teenagers into the conference room. As soon as the senior classmen entered, the police detective started speaking.

"Gentlemen, sit down. We need to talk. You may not know this, but I have been working with the local police force for twenty years. I am considered an expert in gang relations."

"Okay," Luke replied.

"I know all the street signs," he continued. "What you teens found is of grave concern to me. The symbols don't match local markings. They don't represent the gangs in the area."

"Are you sure?" the rookie prodded.

"Trust me, what you discovered is uncommon. I believe that these symbols represent a serious threat."

The school's support staff concurs with me. This situation needs to be addressed by someone outside our local law enforcement."

"What do you mean?" Luke inquired.

Responding the officer continued, "I assure you that we'll complete a thorough investigation, but this circumstance is of national concern."

"What did you say?" the rookie asked.

The investigator replied, "In order to determine the authenticity of these markings, we need assistance from an outside agency. As for right now, we will have to confiscate your cell phones for twenty-four hours. When the investigation is complete, we will call you back to this office."

"What?" Luke shouted. "Not our phones!"

"It is normal school procedure," Mrs. Jones said. "Don't forget you were using them during exam time."

The deputy added, "We will contact your parents to inform them of today's event, so they don't blame you for not having your phones," he promised.

Prompting the teens to leave the room, Mrs. Jones

concluded by saying, "We will call you back into this office tomorrow. That's all that we are going to discuss today, boys. I'll give you each a pass to the library. Solen, you may finish your exam in there."

In bewilderment, Luke and Sol left the administrative building. Still baffled by the onslaught of questioning, the teens shuddered while walking toward the media center.

"This is crazy, bro!" the recruit mused.

"Yeah, it is nuts!" his mentor replied.

"What is going to happen next?"

"I'm not sure. I just want my phone back!"

"It isn't right," the rookie agreed. "It's not cool!"

Within minutes of Sol completing his exam, the final dismissal bell rung. While the X headed home that afternoon, the local law enforcement agency dispatched a squad car. After arriving downtown, the police officers conducted a general analysis. Scoping out the area, the cops located the vacant building and examined the symbols on the fifth floor. Initiating a pictographic translation, the team of officers attempted to decode the message. After failing to do so, the Federal Bureau of Investigation received a call.

"Is this Agent Black?" a local officer requested.

"Yes," a female voice replied.

"We need your assistance in order to expedite a case," the deputy admitted. "This is an elevated priority."

"Provide me more information, and I'll be there in the

morning," she guaranteed. The FBI agent traveled most of the night to get to lend her expertise. Trained in ancient Arabic cartouche, Ms. Black was considered the best in the world at deciphering code.

Walking into the principal's conference room the next morning, Ms. Black asked, "What seems to be the problem?"

After briefing her, the administrative staff called upon Luke and Solen. When the boys entered the executive area, the high ranking official directed each teen toward a chair. "Good morning! I'm Agent Black, but you can call me Ebony."

"Sure," Luke agreed.

"I'm here today to discuss the events that transpired last night."

"What events?" Luke questioned

"First off, I'm aware of the encryption. As a matter of fact, I deciphered the code this morning."

"You did?" the rookie inquired.

"Yes, son, I did," she insisted. "My agency has discovered a small terrorist cell residing in this city. With the help of this encoded message, we narrowed it to one group. After compiling the evidence, the local law enforcement arrested three men last night. Up until that point, I didn't recognize the final piece of this puzzle."

"What puzzle?" Luke interjected.

"Well," Agent Black continued. "After we arrested the three men last night, they confessed to being members of the

Chide. The code is the link to their pending threat. The six-symbol cryptograph is their map. It is the key component to their evil plot."

"But what do the symbols mean?" Sol questioned.

"Yeah, what does it mean?" Luke reiterated.

"One thing at a time, gentlemen. First, you might want to know that Chide intended to unleash an infectious disease upon America."

By now, Agent Black had secured the attention of everyone in the room. In shock, Mrs. Jones replied, "Are you serious?"

Ebony replied, "Yes, with no pun intended, I'm dead serious."

"What if they did?" Luke asked.

Agent Black replied, "If unleashed, the disease would quickly spread, possibly killing hundreds of thousands of Americans. To make matters worse, the Chide planned on carrying out the attack in a large metropolitan city on Christmas day."

"Say what?" Luke objected. "How do you know?"

"Using a state-of-the-art computer system, I entered the information into a database," Agent Black stated. "When I did, the computer relayed the code back within a few minutes. The secret scripted message is a navigational coordinate.

"Where does it lead?" Solen demanded.

"The better question is "what does it mean," Ebony

clarified. Coming to the climax, Agent Black waited for everyone's attention. "The word 'triquetrous' represents a trifold team. The three men are from different regions around the globe. They are a group of three radical criminals gathered together as one. They have a wicked common objective."

"Whoa!" The rookie grimaced.

"The Chide want to take down our country," she swore. "This terrorist cell is evil. Their coordinates suggest that an attack will occur on land, during broad daylight, at last waning crescent moon, and in the month of December. As pertaining to the last month of the year, the Bethlehem star is a no-brainer."

"Oh, I get it," Luke affirmed. "But what about the last symbol?"

"At first, the last pictogram was more difficult to decode," Ebony acknowledged. "It is the sign of Lascaux. Lascaux is a complex array of caves in the southwest of France and has nothing to do with this case. After cross-referencing the name with information from this area, though, I discovered that Lascaux is actually an elite dance club in Miami. It's considered a celebrity bungalow on the corner of Johnson and Riverside Avenue. It's next to the expressway. It will be celebrating its one-year anniversary on Christmas day!" She announced. "Get it?"

"You have got to be kidding me!" Mrs. Jones exclaimed. "You can't be serious?"

"I don't play games," Agent Black assured her seriously. "So, as you can tell, the Chide are a serious threat."

"That is insane!" Solen bellowed.

"Bet!" Luke protested. "This is too much information!"

"Thankfully we squelched the operation and stopped the Chide. We are very fortunate to have intercepted this terrorist plot. With this particular pathogen, people don't get extremely ill for a few days. It takes time to circulate through the body. By the peak of the outbreak, the disease would have already become a national crisis."

"That's insane plotting!" Luke exclaimed.

"That's true evil, man!" Sol agreed.

"You're absolutely correct," Mrs. Jones replied. "I never want to see something like that happen."

"There's true malevolence out there against America," Agent Black said. "Luckily for us, you boys inadvertently assisted in this case. For doing so, I will recommend that both of you receive a hefty reward. You probably didn't realize it, but we pay citizens through our government counterterrorism fund. For bringing these three terrorists to justice, you will be compensated."

"How much money are we taking about?" Luke inquired excitedly.

"You will both each receive twenty thousand dollars!" Ebony proclaimed.

$

Chapter 12
Summer Trip

Upon termination of the meeting, Agent Black debriefed Luke and Solen concerning their capacity to "resume a normal civilian existence."

"Just continue being teenagers," Ebony stated. "It's your responsibility as U.S. citizens to keep everything that has been discussed today confidential. This is all classified information, you understand. Don't talk to anyone."

Both teens agreed.

"You will each receive your reward tomorrow," Ebony Black promised. "The money will be deposited directly into your bank account. Spend it as you wish. Believe it or not, your curiosity and quick wit saved our nation. Thank you for helping solve this case," she concluded.

Ebony then walked out of the room. As soon as she left, Mrs. Jones took over by saying, "Here is a pass back to class and here are your phones. You'll be given extra time to take today's exams to make up for this morning's meeting, but don't forget to keep your phones off this time. Once again, thank you gentlemen for your assistance," praised Mrs. Jones.

Upon being discharged, Luke and Sol headed in opposite directions. When the final bell rang, the team's leader met the rookie in the courtyard, where they recapped the morning's encounter. The teens vowed to each other to keep everything a secret, even from their other friends.

"I won't say a word," the rookie promised. "Anyway, I'm going to jet now. If I don't see you tomorrow, I'll be at your house on Thursday."

"That sounds good," Luke replied. "Peace out, kid!"

Wednesday arrived, ushering in the last day of school. Ready to be unleashed, the teens looked forward to the magnificent voyage to adulthood. After exams, all of the seniors counted down to midday. Right on cue, the official dismissal arrived and the final chime of the bell triggered a grand celebration. As soon as the bell rang, students turned up everywhere. The summer had commenced.

While passing Raven in the hall, Solen shouted, "Hey, congratulations!"

"You too, kid!" she replied, offering best wishes. "Don't forget about tomorrow!"

"I'll be there!" the rookie pledged.

Scattered all across campus, students grooved from one gala to the next during the graduation revelry. Screaming and howling could be heard all over campus.

"Hey, Rocco, it's time to party!" Luke hollered.

"Yes sir, captain!" he replied. "It's time to jam!"

In the background, music played from the school's band members. Previously rehearsed tunes echoed across the grounds as the rock concert began. The intoxicating rhythm led to dancing, and, right down the hall, the student advisory counsel sold refreshments. Between all the festivities, teachers and administrators could only supervise as the events unfolded. In the midst of the harmonic jubilation, the senior classmen ambled toward the exit while confetti flew sky high in an ostentatious departure.

"Good-bye!" Mrs. Jones shouted over the noise. Chuckling at their antics, she yelled, "You better make something of yourselves and not disappoint me!"

The X buzzed along, following the crowd to the parking lot. Before driving away, Luke shouted to his friends, "I'll see everyone tomorrow at my house!" Hyping up the team, he added, "Demark or bust!"

"*Wahoo*!" Raven reacted. "High school is over!"

Moving both arms to breaker mode, Rocco mimicked a robotic voice: "It's time to party!"

"Our graduation ceremony is on Saturday," Gordon reminded.

"Yeah, baby!" Sol hooted. "School is over!"

After a brief farewell, the seniors ventured into the splendid unknown. That evening, while his pals celebrated, Luke worked his magic, finalizing a plan for Copenhagen. After scanning the Web, the X leader set the date and started coordinating a radical trip. Knowing the passports would take time to be processed, he first located a local business that took passport photos.

Next Luke called Solen. Following a brief dialogue, the

traceurs came to a consensus.

"I'll help finance the trip," the rookie promised.

"You pay half and I'll pay half," Luke replied.

Hanging up with Sol, Luke called Blitz Travel.
After conversing with Raven's uncle, he secured airfare for six
people. Before hanging up the telephone, the travel agent also
reserved a room at a five-star hotel in the heart of Copenhagen.

"Aw yeah!" Luke howled. "There's only one thing
missing!"

Conducting another Internet query, the lead traceur
located the perfect vehicle. In a bold statement, Luke secured a
black super stretched limousine.

"We're going to travel in style!" he boasted. "Being
chauffeured is *insane!*"

With everything finalized, he desired to relay a message
to his crew. Embellishing his success, he shouted, "It's time to
text!"

It read, "Congrats, tomorrow we are hitting a new
hotspot!" Then pausing, he continued, "Oh, by the way, we're
booked!"

Waiting ten seconds, he surprised the X with a final note.

"Denmark, August 1. Airfare, limo, hotel, & passports
set! It's Copenhagen or bust!"

Thanks for the photos, Joe!
Cedar Rapids PK is off the chain!
www.crpkmovement.com

Thanks M2 and American Parkour
for the support!
www.americanparkour.com
www.primal-fitness.com
www.tribalmovement.com

I thank the Lord for family, friends, co-workers, teachers, colleagues, students, Tango & Lu, and anyone else that I have forgotten – JFM

Team X

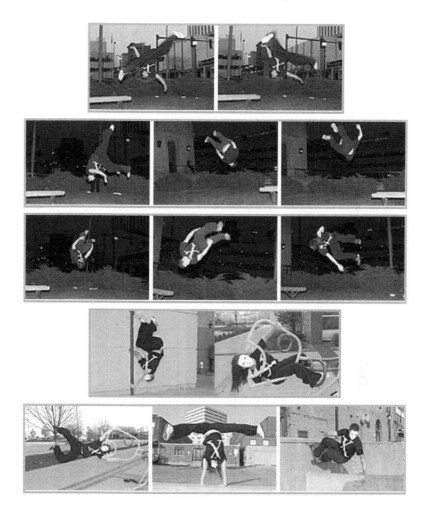

To contact the author, e-mail him at
theparkourcode@gmail.com or visit
theparkourcode.com.

To contact the illustrator, visit his Web site at
ryangallet.com or e-mail him at rgallet@mac.com.

8567857R00065

Printed in Great Britain
by Amazon.co.uk, Ltd.,
Marston Gate.